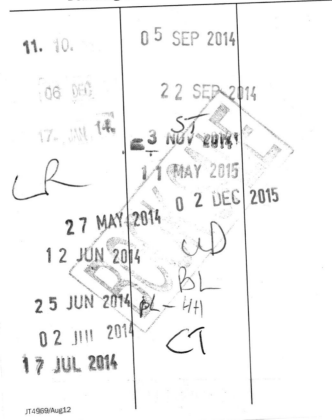

The .45 Goodbye

Outlaw Sonny Boy Clanton had it all: style, courage and a band of pards, loyal to the death. The whole county saw him as a hero – until he kidnapped the Governor's daughter.

Following the uproar, the law, cavalry and citizens scoured the valley for outlaw and hostage, but all in vain.

Then came the quiet rancher who loved the Governor's daughter and would find and save her or die.

W
Clay, Dempsey
.45 goodbye

EG   C70030653-
      £ 12.25

By the same author

Shannon
Five Guns from Diablo
Badlands in My Blood
The Last Hero
A Town Called Limbo
Too Fast to Die
Just Breathin' Hate
Die This Day

The .45 Goodbye

Dempsey Clay

A Black Horse Western

ROBERT HALE · LONDON

ISBN 978-0-7090-8681-9

Robert Hale Limited
Clerkenwell House
Clerkenwell Green
London EC1R 0HT

www.halebooks.com

Typeset by
Derek Doyle & Associates, Shaw Heath
Printed and bound in Great Britain by
CPI Antony Rowe, Chippenham and Eastbourne

CHAPTER 1

THE GOVERNOR'S DAUGHTER

She was expected always to ride within sight of the capital yet she broke that rule virtually every day. Sometimes she would take the black mare far enough south-west to glimpse the remote line of the Panhandle Mountains, while at other times she might explore the twisted canyons and draws of Sundown Flats where men from the territorial capital often hunted coyote, wolf and puma.

Yet mostly Lisa Randolph chose to ride the wide rangeland north of the city, a vast, rolling sweep of open cattle country with its feel of limitless distances and freedom.

She'd dreamed of country just like this during her careful, protected upbringing in the cities of the east, and since coming to South-west Territory to rejoin her father, the governor, three months earlier, felt she simply couldn't get enough of it. With her spun-gold hair streaming out behind and with her perfect seat in the saddle and the glow of youth lighting her lovely, eighteen-year-old face, she seemed a natural part of this wild, free land.

She certainly appeared like some kind of vision to the five outlaws sprawled full length in the deep brush flanking the horse trail two miles north of Dinnebito Wash.

To the eyes of such men whose women were largely of the shopworn variety to be found in border dives or remote trailhouses, the governor's daughter was vividly different from anything they had ever seen before.

Even Sonny Boy Clanton whose plan it was to abduct the governor's daughter, was seen to stare and shake his curly head in admiration and surprise. He'd heard that Lisa Randolph was a genuine looker yet somehow the glowing reality of her riding towards him unawares now made that description seem inadequate.

Lisa rode with her gaze fixed upon the west where the slanting sun was spilling down the slopes of the distant mountains, tingeing their flanks with colour.

A smile played about her mouth as she watched a falcon rise from the trees off to her left.

The bird caught the hot thermals and went sailing eastward, swiftly rising to a thousand feet then gliding off towards the distant city. Majestic and remote, the predator sailed high over sun-bleached rooftops and crowded streets. Its shadow fell fleetingly across the gloomy high walls of the governor's palace where a silver-headed man with Lisa's blue eyes and broad brow sat labouring over letters and documents, too busy even to glance up and enjoy the soaring flight of a falcon in the sun.

A pensive look crossed the girl's face as she approached a brushy section of the trail. She was thinking of her father and how angry he would be should he discover she'd disobeyed his orders every afternoon. She wondered idly if he could still remember what it had been like to be young and restless – before he'd become shackled to responsibility.

She sighed.

All that never-ending duty involved in ruling a half-wild section of the great West which seemed intent on fighting responsibility and civilization with the same fierce energy with which it had once battled the Indians. . . .

She shrugged the thought aside. She tried never to allow serious matters to intrude upon these hours of stolen enjoyment. The black mare tossed her head with pleasure when the girl reached down to pat the glossy neck – and in that instant it became dramatically over-crowded along that section of the brush-flanked trail just north of Dinnebito Wash.

Dick Rutherford got to the mare first to seize it by the head harness. The young hellion flashed a cockily reassuring grin as the girl gasped in fright.

'Now don't get het up, Miss Randolph,' he told her. 'We ain't aimin' to hurt you none.'

'That's so, missy,' insisted shock-haired Fritz Lincoln with a grin. Lincoln grinned most of the time; he'd been known to blast a man out of his boots with his Colt without losing that wide, toothy smile.

Her shock giving way to fury now, Lisa lifted her riding crop but lithe Marlon Lord moved in swiftly to pull her arm down. As Pomeroy snatched the crop from her fingers a voice snapped from behind:

'Go easy, Brick. This ain't one of your ugly sluts, man!'

Pomeroy flushed hotly and Lisa whirled in the saddle to stare down at Sonny Boy Clanton.

She instantly knew it was the outlaw, though she didn't recognize any of the others. Only the leader's smiling handsome features ornamented true bills all across Deaf Smith County.

But he was just a boy!

8

That was her first stunned impression. Of course, everybody knew the outlaw was just twenty-one years old, yet his pictures made him appear older. He was not tall yet carried himself ramrod-erect. He was dressed in shotgun chaps, Star boots and a vivid yellow shirt. A Stetson was worn tilted back, his slim waist was encircled by a double gun rig. There was something sinister about those big Colt revolvers yet the man's youthful countenance appeared innocent by contrast.

Sunny Boy Clanton was the name on the wanted posters – rustler, gunfighter, killer. They said he'd shot his first man at fifteen and now at twenty-one appeared to have become some kind of symbol of wild western youth. Many of his reckless breed had died, quit or simply vanished before the onslaught of the new laws which had come with the first governor supported by the feared territorial militia. Yet Clanton had somehow survived, simply doing as he'd always done. It seemed he robbed where he chose, killed those who came after him and thus far had defied all attempts to bring him to justice.

Now he smiled, which only appeared to add to his patently phony air of innocence.

'Right from the jump I've got to tell you there ain't nothing personal about this, Miss Lisa,' he assured her. 'I've got nothing against your daddy – other than that he stands on the opposite side of the fence and is always trying to kill me, that is. You reckon you can believe I don't aim to harm you none?'

Standing stiffly in the dappled tree shadow, Lisa stared around at the silent horsemen encircling her and knew real fear. Yet when her attention returned to the leader she felt that sensation begin to dissipate, which didn't even begin to make sense. After several confusing moments she realized she sensed in Clanton a hint of gentleness that was surely at odds with his reputation. She was startled to hear her own voice sound so calm.

'Why, I rather think I do believe you, Sonny.'

It was the outlaw's turn to appear startled. Then he laughed suddenly and winked at his henchmen. 'Hey, did you hear that, *amigos*? The governor's daughter – and yet she's ready to take the word of badass Sonny Boy.'

None of his henchmen responded. These were desperate men, long hounded and hunted by the law over crimes which could lead them all to the grave or the gallows. Not even easy-going Fritz Lincoln could manage an answering smile.

'These boys always fuss and fret too much, Miss Lisa,' Clanton stated, turning back to the girl. 'I've been able to teach them not to be scared of the rope, the gun or the goddamn law – but for some reason I've never been able to cure them of fretting about the future.'

He laughed softly yet was sober in a second as he spread leather-chapped legs wide and folded both arms across his chest.

'Well, enough of that, let's get down to cases. You see, Miss Lisa, the truth of it is, your daddy is causing us plenty grief lately, what with his militiamen running us ragged and those big rewards he's got posted. So I just decided I'd have to do something about it. You know, like, spike his guns? And that's what I aim to do now . . . with your help.'

She lifted her chin. 'And how could I possibly assist someone like you, Mr Outlaw?'

'Why, simple as winking,' came the ready reply. 'All you got to do is camp out with me and the boys a spell. And before you start fretting about that I'll tell you no harm is going to come to you while you're under my protection. That ain't the way I operate. You see, now I'm holding you I mean to convince your daddy, see that me and him gotta come to an understanding about the future . . . you know, live and let live kinda thing? As soon as that's done I'll escort you back home safe and sound, and after that you and yours truly are both going to get to sleep a lot whole better nights. Savvy?'

'You're saying you're kidnapping me in order to force my father to stop hunting you?'

'Right.'

'You're wasting your time.'

11

'I never waste my time.'

'You are now. You see, Mr Clanton, my father was sent out here to clean out the lawless elements and make the territory a safe place for people to live. The President personally gave him his instructions and he made a vow to carry them out. You don't know my father. Once he sets his mind to something he won't allow anything to deter him until the job is completed.'

'This time things are different.' Clanton spoke slowly, eyes distant now. 'You see, Miss Lisa, I know just how a man feels when he loves somebody who's pretty and helpless . . . and that somebody is in danger. . . .'

His face had turned cold, frighteningly so.

'Oh, yeah,' he whispered, 'that I surely know. . . .'

'Sonny,' she said urgently. Then she hesitated. 'May I call you that?'

His white smile flashed. 'Why, surely.'

'Don't do this. It won't get you what you want . . . and somehow I feel you're not really that sort of person who wants to be involved in a kidnapping. Oh, yes, I know all the terrible things people say about you. But having met you I simply can't see you in the role of a merciless killer . . . or somebody who would kidnap a defenceless girl, if it comes to that. You simply don't.'

The outlaw studied her for so long in a kind of

12

puzzled silence that brooding Marlon Lord was finally moved to interject.

'Judas, Sonny, are we gonna stand around here jawboning until mebbe a whole regiment of troopers shows up through the tall grass? Let's get moving, man!'

Clanton made a vague gesture without taking his eyes from the girl. 'I'm still running this show.' Then, to Lisa, 'You know, I get the crazy feeling you mean what you just said.'

'I do,' she replied honestly. 'Every word.'

The outlaws traded questioning looks. They were desperadoes trained to hit fast then vanish. They realized the governor's daughter was a true beauty with a charm to match, but didn't see that as reason why they should take the risk of further delay. They were only a few miles from Capital City, for Pete's sake!

'Hmmm!' Clanton muttered, massaging his smooth-shaven jaw and studying the girl thoughtfully. 'Mebbe I should—'

'Johnny, I know what you're thinking,' Lord cut in harshly. 'Well, forget it, man. This ain't Kate. She is the governor's daughter and she could get us our pardon. That's all. End of story!'

Lisa looked from one man to the other. 'What is he talking about, Sonny? Who is Kate?'

Clanton's brow was furrowed and a look of naked

13

pain crossed his face. 'My sister Kate. She was just about your age . . . and she looked like you and you even talk alike.'

'Oh, then you have a sister, Johnny?'

'Had!'

The outlaw leader's tone was suddenly harsh and rough-edged. He dragged the back of his hand across his mouth and turned bleakly to his gun *segundo*. 'I dunno, Mar. Mebbe this whole damned idea of ours was—'

'Was right from the jump, and still is,' Lord cut in. 'We've been planning this for a long spell now and you know it's the only sure way to get the governor off our necks.'

'Only way,' affirmed Brick Pomeroy, and the others nodded in agreement.

Lisa felt her heart sink as she watched the gang boss struggle with himself. Finally he sighed. 'I guess you are right, boys.' He gave the girl a wan smile. 'Sorry, Lisa.'

She made to protest but the change in Clanton's manner silenced her, causing her to realize her brief moment of advantage had come and gone. The outlaw now appeared remote and dangerous, the Clanton of the newspapers and wanted dodgers. Yet because of something she'd seen in the man she was no longer afraid. This enabled her to lift her chin and appear unconcerned as she watched them affix

14

a sheet of note paper to the mare's saddle before sending it off with a slap to the hindquarters, to be picked up eventually by the searchers who would surely soon come.

Then, mounted behind Clanton with her arms linked about his slender waist, she rode off into the hills as sunset came down over Deaf Smith County.

The three horsemen came down out of the Wolftail Hills onto the moon-silvered benchlands of the Split Spur Ranch. They rode boldly like honest men instead of what they really were – thieves with their eyes on a bunch of prime steers.

Ridge, Kehoe and Peacock had been watching the little cow spread all day. An hour earlier they'd sighted the youthful rancher riding off towards town togged out in his best Sunday rig. Kehoe had promptly dispatched Ridge around by the butte overlooking the town trail, and when the man reported back that Vallery was indeed on the trail for distant Buffalo Hump it was like an invitation to go to work.

This was familiar territory for lanky Ridge and bow-legged Peacock, for they were small-time badmen who had plied their trade in the territory for years in between time spent behind bars.

Leader Drum Kehoe was a ruthless cut above. A hard-bodied man of thirty with eyes like bullets, he'd come to the county to steal, and meeting hardcases

Ridge and Peacock by chance back in the cattle country he had made a quick decision to go rustling.

'Easy pickings,' insisted Ridge as they spotted the cattle through the woods ahead, munching buffalo grass. 'Good condition, too. Should fetch top price across in the Wolftails, boys.'

'Easier than shoving your snout into a bank, eh, Drum?' remarked Peacock.

Kehoe maintained a broody silence. He hated cows and regarded rustling as penne ante stuff. But he was in no position to be choosy.

'I'll cut across over yonder to that ridge and keep lookout while you fellers round 'em up,' he said. 'Get moving!'

Ridge and Peacock didn't like their partner but let him give the orders. They set about their work quickly, rounding up the stock while Kehoe stood watch higher up. No trouble showed, and when his partners signalled to him, Kehoe rode down and dropped in behind men and cattle to ride rear guard with his .45 in his fist.

The operation continued smooth as silk as they drove the stolen cavvy away through a series of narrow fissures in the hills to the east of the spread, then hustled them on through the rough country for several swift miles. With that stretch behind them they guided the cavvy across a stretch of flinty limestone country which left no tracks, then swung south-

16

west for Hackett's Gap.

Good time continued to be made as they travelled on westwards through the night and it was still black dark when the heavens opened up and continued to deluge down like it might never quit. By the time daylight finally broke across the wide rangelands, grey and drear, it appeared as if the stone jaws of Wolftail Pass had opened up overnight and swallowed Dev Vallery's little cow herd whole.

CHAPTER 2

THE GUN AGAIN

'Brotherly love!' proclaimed Preacher Henry Peck from the pulpit of his brand new church. With bony hands gripping the edge of the lectern he glared imperiously out over the congregation. 'Fraternal love, the only virtue that can bring true peace to the wilderness, hope to the human heart, and pure joy to the eye of the Creator!'

The congregation soaked it up even though Preacher Peck was a far better veterinarian than part-time parson. Tonight, just about anybody could have held their interest for this was the opening service at Buffalo Hump's fine new place of worship.

They had built it themselves: storekeepers, ranchers, cowboys, clerks, women and children. Long before its completion the church had come to be a symbol of a new, law-abiding way of life in this remote section of Deaf Smith County. Everybody who'd played any part in the church's construction had turned up tonight, most to be seen and a few even to hear the Word.

And the Word tonight was brotherly love.

'Love thy neighbour,' insisted grim Henry Peck, who'd not spoken to next-door neighbour Mick Pollock in three bitter years. 'Embrace him, shower him with kindness.' He sucked in a deep breath. 'Forgive him his sins – no matter what the varmint might have done to you in the past!'

It seemed to Dev Vallery seated in the pew three rows from the back beside Sheriff Harvey Shield, that Peck's eye fell directly upon him as he delivered that last sentence.

His smile was tolerant for he didn't expect anybody to forget his past in just six months. It would surely take Buffalo Hump longer to forget completely that Dev Vallery had once been a youthful partner of the now notorious Sonny Boy Clanton.

Yet there were encouraging signs here and he sensed many now believed he'd hung up the irons for good and wanted nothing more out of life than to raise cows and keep his nose clean. Of course it would take some longer to forget. It always did.

He was lucky he didn't look like any kind of wild one at twenty-three years of age, with regular open features dominated by a head of thick black hair, and nowadays he rarely even packed a Colt. He was occasionally sighted taking a drink with the sheriff and it seemed half the unmarried girls in town had set their caps for him.

Of course some would take longer to accept his reformation than others, and he was reminded of this outside the church following the service when the formidable Miss Pringle paused to remark, 'Well, Mr Vallery, I must say I never expected to see you inside a church!' then sniffed and was off in a swirl of petticoats, radiating disapproval.

'Don't pay any mind to that old biddy, Dev,' Sheriff Harvey Shield wheezed, joining him on the lawn. 'Hell, just last week she was at me to arrest Barry Gunn for spitting on the sidewalk. Nobody measures up to that one's standards.'

Vallery just shrugged, yet found himself reflecting on the past when he was finally riding home. Nobody here knew anything about his tough childhood or his growing years when only a six-gun and an ice-cold nerve prevented him from starving to death on the cruel streets of the West.

But all here knew he'd once been part of the wild bunch sometimes known as 'The Sonny Boys' who had raised plenty hell back in the past.

He'd quit the old life cold and reckoned it had been just in time. For while he'd spent a year proving to the world he was a reformed character, Clanton had been on a steady slide from reckless hellraiser to cattle rustler, gun hellion and enemy of the law.

Vallery rarely reflected upon the past these days, and with his own land beneath him an hour later it was impossible not to feel good. Soon the familiar surrounds of rolling grasslands and the smell of the river had expelled all else from his thoughts.

The Split Spur Ranch was just a half-section but every acre was top grade cattle country and with Weeping Woman River wending through it, water was never a problem.

He'd first sighted the land two years back when riding back from some reckless adventure in the north with Sonny Boy. From that day onwards he'd planned secretly to give up the gun and settle down to raise beef, but didn't see how he could do it, with his record, until Randolph came to South-west Territory as governor and brought with him a strange new word.

Amnesty.

The wild ones of Deaf Smith County were quick to learn that amnesty meant a clean slate for every lawbreaker prepared to stand up before the governor, place his right hand upon the Bible and swear never to break the law again – so help me God!

Clanton had scoffed at the whole concept and Dev Vallery more or less did likewise. Then it happened –

when the governor himself, aware both of his notoriety and charisma, had actually sought Vallery out in prison to offer him the same terms as any other wild one should he swear the oath to live within the law and give up the old ways . . . before it was too late.

To the shock and disbelief of many, he'd seized the opportunity with both hands and had never looked back as he set about improving his reputation and playing down his friendship with Clanton.

A short time later Randolph made the huge promise either to clean up the gangs entirely or tender his resignation.

The man was still governor eighteen months on, and Dev Vallery was now listed on the county electoral role as 'rancher' and no longer 'gunman'.

He was riding along, grinning and reflecting when he suddenly drew rein. He was crossing his own home acres now but realized he couldn't see his herd.

For a long moment he simply sat his saddle staring off at the south pasture where the stock usually grazed this time of day.

Nothing. . . .

He was alarmed for a moment then quickly reassured himself most likely he'd find they'd strayed over across the broken-backed ridge to the clover patches beyond, or maybe had taken to the timber for some unfathomable bovine reason of their own?

But the stock wasn't across the ridge nor hiding amongst the trees.

It was some twenty minutes later before he drew rein and faced reality. His stock had been stolen. Which meant he was, of that moment, facing almost certain ruin!

The moment stretched into a frozen minute which might likely prove one of the most momentous of his whole life.

He'd foresworn the gun and this had proven surprisingly easy. Yet staring unseeingly over the section where his cattle should have been, he knew just two things. He had to go after the rustlers – and that a man never went after rustlers without a gun.

Vivid memories of the day he'd packed the .45 away for keeps flashed before his eyes. A tremor ran through him, he cursed, and then was wheeling the big horse to go storming across the pastures for the headquarters at a headlong gallop.

Somewhere during that swift ride the quiet-living young cattleman disappeared and the one-time rider of the owlhoot trails filled his shoes.

It was a grim young man who leapt down at the house and lunged through the front room into the galley to reach for the flat cedar box which lay atop the bureau behind the kitchen door.

His hands were upon the lid of the box when he caught his reflection in wall mirror. The small square of glass was just big enough to encompass a pale, tight-lipped face and glittering grey eyes.

Instantly he set the box down and stepped back from it, hands no longer steady. This weapon would always be a reminder of those years when he'd worn the tag the newspapers had handed him – Fast Dev – one of the best of the guntippers. He'd sworn the day he'd come here that he would never wear the Colt again unless there was no other way.

Was there another way here?

He considered briefly, shook his dark head. Should he ride to town for the sheriff? By the time a posse was formed his cattle could be clear across the county line where a smart rustler would have a dozen run-out trails to choose from in the wild country.

He must go after them alone, right now, and he must take his gun. . . .

Refusing to meeting his eyes in the looking glass he snapped open the box and lifted out the coiled gun rig. It was cool, heavy and all-too familiar to his touch. He remained staring at nothing for a frozen strip of time before suddenly uncoiling the rig and swiftly buckling it around narrow hips, knotting the rawhide thong around his right thigh.

He slipped the Peacemaker from leather, checked the loads perfunctorily then drove the piece back

24

into the cutaway holster.

Delaying only long enough to scribble a brief note in the event of long absence, he legged it outside, slammed the door in back of him and sprang into the saddle.

He struck out directly for the Wolftail Hills. He had ridden the rustler trails himself and knew exactly on which route he would take a herd of primes from this quarter.

He was neither surprised nor disappointed when he failed to pick up any sign as he pounded southwest through thinning timber. He was taking the shortest possible route for Coyote Pass which he hoped to make in daylight – but eventually darkness fell like a club.

Still a mile short of his objective he reined in, jumped down in a mesquite grove and started in scratching matches into life on his chaps and inspecting the terrain. He'd used up maybe a dozen before match-light revealed the stone. It was an ordinary chunk of quartz about the size of a fist, but its upper side was darker and damper than the side it was resting upon, which could only mean it had been recently overturned.

Old memories stirred. He knew what it was like to steal stock then work frantically at erasing the sign on your run-out. He and Sonny Boy had been expert at this in the old days, and he knew the thieves would never have left something as obvious as that behind them had they been aware of it.

It was like an arrow pointing out the direction they had taken.

He scouted about with renewed energy and soon located a clear hoof print in soft soil, angling south. Due south lay the old Kiowa Trail which crossed the county line down at Silleck's Pass.

Back in the saddle he set off at headlong pace through deepening darkness until the first stars winked out to guide him along the ridge line which in turn took him to the shallow crossing at Owl Creek then upwards over Buffalo Hump as the moon finally broke loose of the high country hills to light his way. The light revealed cattle tracks stretching away before him along with fresh droppings and the sharper prints left by three shod ponies.

He forced himself to relax for the first time in two hours when he reined up on a knoll to fashion a cigarette. He lighted up and drew deep with grim satisfaction. Now he knew how many men were involved, the route they had taken, and where they were headed.

The thieves had made several minor mistakes and one major one. They had rustled from an ex-rustler.

Prodded awake by dawn's first weak light the cattle began to stir. The thieves rose stiffly from the bedrolls where they'd spent several hours of moonless night, resting yet not sleeping. They scratched and yawned but didn't speak much as they set about saddling up. They had covered hard miles overnight, yet there was still a good stretch ahead before reaching Hackett's Gap and the pay-off.

As befitted the top man, Drum Kehoe sat his paint off to one side and fashioned a rice-paper cigarette while Peacock and Ridge got the reluctant herd moving. Kehoe was a little stiff from the night's punishing journey through the hill country and would have paid a silver dollar for a good mug of coffee. Yet overall he was feeling pretty content and self-satisfied until his gaze drifted casually backtrail.

A thin column of dust was climbing the still morning air less than a mile behind.

Freezing in the act of raising the cigarette to his lips, the rustler blinked, cursed then snatched field glasses from his saddle-bag.

'Judas Priest!' he hissed as the shape of horse and rider emerged from the timbered hill. Then he filled his lungs and bellowed, 'Someone's on our hammer. Take cover and get ready to take the bastard down!'

The way Ridge and Peacock reacted revealed a lot about the kind of badmen they were in comparison with their leader. They were thieves and jailbirds, but not killers. In truth they had an unspoken agreement between them always to flee sooner than fight, and instinct saw both men swing away from the slow-moving bunch and point their horses' heads south, poised to run.

Kehoe had other ideas.

'Stand fast, you yellow sons of bitches!' he snarled and was waving a six-hooter in their direction when the sharp click of hoof against stone caused him to hip around in his saddle. All colour drained from hawk features when he saw the tall horseman erupt from cover to come boiling down the rock-littered slope almost within six-gun range.

'Follow me and take cover!' he bawled and heeled his horse for a stand of trailside boulders. For a moment it seemed the others might cut and run, as they surely craved to do. But they were too close to Kehoe and too scared of the man to risk flight. Instead they raked with spurs to storm away down trail towards the boulders at the gallop.

A six-gun blasted from up-slope.

'Hold up, thieves!' the fast-moving rider hollered. 'Next shot, I won't aim to miss!'

As the protecting boulders engulfed Ridge he snatched a glance over his shoulder, and cursed. 'Judas Priest! I figgered he looked familiar. That there yonder is Dev Vallery. I seen him in town Saturday night when we stopped off.'

'The hell you say!' Kehoe was off his horse and brandishing his shooter. The name 'Vallery' was less notorious than it had been once but still carried weight. Yet Kehoe had true grit which showed as he lunged past the uncertain pair. 'C'mon, it's still three-to-one . . . and we're gunners and he's just a sod-busting used-to-be!'

This exhortation worked for Peacock, and the lean badman was hard on Kehoe's heels, before glancing back to see his henchman heading off in the opposite direction.

'Yellow sonova—' he began, then threw himself full length behind a granite outcropping as Kehoe's Colt thundered twice, one slug screaming away in a vicious ricochet off rock.

Hot lead answered and the rustlers dropped to their knees behind cover in time to see a tall figure come out of his saddle and instantly vanish in the timber almost within spitting distance across the trail.

With a curse Kehoe raked the rancher's position with a volley of thundering shots. Vallery touched off but a single shot in reply then dropped belly flat to go snaking away in the long grass. As Kehoe raised his second gun and fired blindly in hope of scoring a lucky shot, Vallery worked his way behind heavy cover growth that enabled him to rise in a crouch and pin-point the enemy's position.

His face set like stone as he raised his hot Colt. He had no real stomach for this work. But past experience had taught him that at such times a man mostly had but two choices – fight or die. And he was not about to die.

Deliberately he lined up on the enemy's position and squeezed off three evenly spaced shots. He was rewarded by a sharp howl of pain and a sudden flurry of blurring movement. Then, as the day's first bars of sunlight came cutting down over the slopes through wisping cordite smoke, they afforded him a momentary glimpse of two indistinct figures rushing back in the direction of the horses.

'Hold up, thieves!' he roared, springing erect. 'I said—'

A figure whirled and triggered. It was a brilliant shot from Kehoe the outlaw. Vallery felt the hissing air whip of a lethal two ounces of lead so close to his neck he actually felt the heat of it. And the rustler was readying to trigger again.

Vallery beat him to it. His gun roared and Kehoe's shot went straight up in the sky as the outlaw reeled away sideways clutching at his chest to topple over a spur of greystone and dropped from sight.

For a moment the surviving rustler offered a perfect target, locked where he stood and frozen by fear with his unshaved horse – face drained of all colour.

'Reach!'

Vallery's shout spurred the the rustler into violent

action, hurdling a boulder and vanishing in shoulder-high brush leaving the rancher standing there with his Colt cocked and the single thought running through his mind: Surely one dead man is enough, Vallery?

The fading sounds of running footsteps ceased abruptly, to be followed moments later by the sharp clatter of a horse starting up.

Convinced it was over now Vallery began to run swiftly downslope casting about for his horse. which he finally glimpsed through the timber. He quickly calmed the animal with a soothing word and moments later was back in the saddle.

With the advantage of the additional height he spotted the bobbing backs of his beeves rushing away down a rock-littered slope in the middle distance. He dropped low over the animal's neck and touched horsehide with spur.

He didn't even see the bloodied, ashen-faced figure of Drum Kehoe rise swaying and ghost-like from a tumbled rock pile with a cocked Colt in his fist and a madness in the eye. The .45 roared thunderously and Vallery flinched as hot pain scorched his left forearm.

Instantly he triggered back and saw his bullet smash home with an impact that hurled the man backwards to vanish in the smoke of his own gun.

Grim and white jawed now, Vallery leaned low over

the horse's neck and was swiftly gone, quickly reaching full gallop along the down-sloping trail in the wake of the stampede.

The herd ran blindly for thirty minutes before Vallery was finally able to swing them into a box canyon. For some time the critters milled about wildly, yet settled quickly enough after he'd closed off the entrance with deadfalls and brush.

It was only then that he realized how utterly quiet it had suddenly become. It remained so when he turned to gaze up to sight the sinister shapes of three buzzards already flapping purposefully westwards towards the site of the gunfight.

His shirt was soaked in sweat and caked by dust. He became aware, belatedly, his tobacco was damp yet he really craved a smoke. He wasn't surprised to find his hands were shaking, for Dev Vallery, cattle rancher and former wild rider, had never killed a white man before.

He drew smoke deep into his lungs and let it spill out over his lower lip. The cattle stared dumbly at him from beyond their barricade. A grey lizard that refused to be disturbed by the early morning turmoil where it lay basking upon a slab of red stone nearby fixed the man with an unblinking stare. Briefly, he had the feeling the eyes of the whole world was focused upon Dev Vallery in silent accusation. . . .

He shrugged, drew deeply again and that feeling

was swiftly gone. Thieves had attempted to take what was his and he'd fought them off as was his right. There could be no guilt attached to that.

His fingers were steady as he reloaded the Peacemaker and slid it back into the holster.

Clambering onto a lookout rock he stood drawing on his smoke and watching the now silent slope behind. Three men had jumped him, he'd killed one and two escaped. The Vallery of just one year earlier would have known exactly what to do in such a situation. First make sure the cattle were secure then mount and go after the other two to shoot it out – kill both if needs be. There was still enough of the old Vallery left in him for this course of action to appeal, he realized. Yet there was no way he would succumb to it. The new Vallery didn't think like that any more.

An hour later with horse and cattle rested and calmed, he drove his herd down out of the high country. He watered them at a spring then set off along an easy, roundabout route that would take him north of the Wolftail Hills beyond the landmark of Monument Butte. Sometime after midnight he was back home on Split Spur.

He had survived and had his cattle back. He was content with that and would leave retribution to others.

CHAPTER 3

NIGHT RIDER

The lone rider crossed an ancient land, a landscape of broken buttes and shattered stone towers looming above all the familiar tumbling vastness he'd seen in turn blistered by summer's heat and frozen by winter's cold.

Dust lifted sluggishly from the hoofs of his dun-coloured horse and the sun fell hot across his shoulders. Yet by the time he had reached his destination far to the west the world would be dark and chill again save for the lamps and blazing brands ringing the high walls of Capital City which illuminated the city enclosed beyond.

From a distance the city resembled a vast mass of dark stone and clay which might well have somehow

34

been thrust up under subterranean pressure from the bowels of the earth to loom broodingly over this wide, semi-desert sweep of the plains. But as the heat haze shimmered and began to fade the distinctive shapes and structures of a sprawling walled city, dating back to a primitive architectural style that had been the south-western fashion many decades before America's great rush West, was revealed before him.

Sonny Boy Clanton felt his spine tingle with excitement as he selected one of a number of deeply rutted roads which reached outwards from beneath the high arched gateways of the city like spokes on a giant wheel.

With swarms of armed scouts and troopers currently scattered far and wide in search of the governor's daughter and her outlaw captor at the moment, and the city itself bristling nervously with guns from wall to wall, here he was riding alone and undisguised into the enemy stronghold with an unlighted cigarette dangling from his lips and a battered black hat tugged low to engulf his face in deepest shadow.

There was nothing to be achieved by this reckless display of bravado beyond the feeding of his own vanity and the exhilaration danger always gave him.

If he had a single goal in mind it was simply to prove his courage to himself and to display his total contempt for his enemies.

Or maybe he just intended to make the governor
– already heavily under fire from many for having
failed to prevent this disaster with his daughter –
appear even further humiliated and weakened.

Each arched entry gate was heavily guarded by big-
hatted figures with rifles, but none challenged the
slim shabby figure astride the dusty dun as he plod-
ded beneath the outer wall half an hour before
midnight. Weary eyes vaguely noted this one
appeared not much more than a boy and sported no
visible arms. They would conserve their time and
energy in the event somebody who looked like real
trouble should arrive even though nobody believed
there was any prospect of that.

The government might be in crisis at the moment,
but so far as anybody from the governor down to the
water boys was concerned, there could not possibly
be any threat to Capital City itself, least of all from
any rag-tail bunch of gun boys from the wild country
away to the south-east in the tumbledown
Panhandles.

As he entered the city proper the rider cut sharp
eyes left at the vast sprawl of the army horse yards. He
nodded with satisfaction on seeing the high-railed
yards were virtually empty, which told him Randolph
still had large numbers of cavalrymen taking part in
the massive manhunt for his daughter and her

captors. What he was seeing reassured him that the enemy was finally taking him seriously and his chest puffed with pride as he crossed the cobbled Plaza Pueblo.

Above him now, upon the low roofs, crouched old three-pounder cannons with yawning black muzzles which had been winched up there in the wake of the massacre of the old governor several years earlier. The outlaw sneered. They were so neglected and way out of date, too rusty even to swing open their breeches. But at least they still looked like guns, he supposed.

To reach the Square of Heroes he was forced to ride past several further sentry posts where sullen figures in uniforms glanced up at the sounds of his passing then turned back to their low-burning fires.

Just another ragged-assed nobody, they thought – and so several uneventful minutes later saw him finally enter the Square of Heroes.

The bulky structure directly before him was called a palace but was in reality just an ugly grey four-floored edifice of stone and cement encircled by high guarded walls fifteen feet high by three deep.

The governor's palace and, until recently, his daughter's safe home.

Governor Randolph was widely popular yet still had enough enemies to warrant security was maintained here day and night.

A sentry pacing the high parapets cast a bored stare down at this hunched rider making his way towards the palace's front gates through the restless grey ranks of the city's night people, the gamblers, thieves and whores, the sleepless and the homeless along with the dangerous ones amongst whom this slender mounted figure beneath the big battered hat looked like just another loser.

The rider touched fingers to hatbrim in a lazy salute upwards and the lookout grunted and continued on his patrol of the parapets.

Swinging down at a hitchrail, Clanton tied up and set off to stroll along the length of the palace's brooding front wall. He laughed in the shadow of his hat envisioning Randolph's chagrin were he to realize the man responsible for rocking his whole world was passing by below within fifty yards of his bedchamber, and now had actually paused to scrape a vesta against the very wall of his palace.

He found what he was looking for. The clapboard Petition Box was set in the wall alongside a guarded gate. The box was one of the governor's ideas to encourage closer contact with the people. All were free to praise or condemn, but the brief note Clanton slipped into the slot simply contained a threat:

Call off the manhunt or I will not be responsible
for Lisa's safety.

S.B.C

A step sounded close behind!

He whirled with right hand wrapping around
gunbutt, ready for anything. A hulking bum
approached clutching a sorry straw hat out before
him.

'Gimme a dollar!' It wasn't a request but a
demand.

'Why, I'm sorry all to hell but if you want something off me you're just going to have to come and
take it – you sorry horse's ass!' Sonny Boy said, and
grinned.

The bum blinked and lunged forward, only to be
smashed unconscious by a savage blow from the butt
of a .45 that opened his simian brow.

The panhandler dropped as though pole-axed.
Before the bystanders could figure what had
happened the slim figure had legged it back to his
mount and vaulted into the saddle to go trotting off
through the night walkers.

This was crazy and he knew it. Yet Sonny Boy
Clanton appeared the calmest man on the Square of
Heroes as uproar began to break out well behind him
now, and somebody howled, 'Hey, guards, somebody
just busted up a man over yonder by the palace wall!'

Within moments, soldiers bristling with arms came spilling from a barracks gateway and didn't even spare a second look for the innocent-looking rider heading casually for the outer gates astride an unremarkable horse.

Soon the entryway to the long dark street lay before him, wide open and inviting.

He galloped its length without hindrance then cut back to a leisurely walk approaching the first set of gates beyond. With hat tilted forward to conceal his face he swayed in the saddle like a drunk and yelled a slurred obscenity at the sentry posted by a glowing brazier when the man made a half-hearted move to challenge him. He saw the man hesitate a moment and in that chink of time he raked the dun with steel and dropped low over its neck when it broke into a gallop.

A single shout followed by a high warning shot followed him before he swung around the first corner, still unscathed and suppressing laughter. Instantly he cut back to a trot to pass unhurriedly by a pair of sentries by the outer gates. They barely spared him a glance before turning back to their glowing brazier and stretched hands out to the warmth while speculating on what the rumpus within the city might be about.

'I play with death!' Sonny Boy Clanton chuckled breathlessly and was swallowed by darkness.

*

Dev Vallery was puzzled.

Having reached town late that morning with a body lashed across his horse, which he'd duly delivered to the undertaker, he'd naturally presented himself at the jailhouse to give a recounting of events to the law.

But if Sheriff Harvey Shield was even remotely interested in the overnight bloodletting out in the Wolftail Hills he gave no sign.

The only thing different about his visitor today from the badgeman's point of view, was that Dev was wearing a Colt strapped to his hip. Vallery had no desire to go manhunting but would feel obliged to do so if Shield should so request.

The rancher had attracted some curious faces on his journey here from the undertaker's for this was the first time Buffalo Hump had seen him wearing a Colt since his return a year ago now.

Harvey Shield studied the younger man. Vallery had arrived a year earlier armed with a letter of reference from Governor Randolph explaining that the former wild rider had accepted amnesty from the law. He was now considered by the governor to be reformed and worthy of the sheriff's confidence and support, so the report had assured.

One year on, the crusty sheriff had come to hold

the young rancher in genuine regard, and they had become friends.

So how come the sheriff now appeared almost indifferent about an attempted rustling and a shooting?

At last Shield seemed to grow aware of his puzzlement.

'Er, yeah,' he rumbled, then bent to open a drawer and withdrew a newspaper which he shoved across the desk. 'I take it you haven't seen this?'

Frowning, Dev picked up the copy of the *Capital City Sentinel* bearing the banner headline.

GOVERNOR'S DAUGHTER ABDUCTED!

He felt the colour drain from his face.

'What the hell—?'

'Better read it all, Dev.'

Vallery's eyes swept over the printed page and he felt his blood chill when he read the name, 'Sonny Boy Clanton'. The report revealed that Lisa Randolph had been abducted by Clanton while riding north of Capital City on the previous Tuesday afternoon. The girl's horse, later found by searchers, had a note attached warning Governor Randolph to expect to hear more from the outlaw in due course.

'Sonny Boy . . . goddamnit! What the hell—?'

'Hit you pretty hard, eh, Dev? Figured it would.'

Vallery was unable to respond as segments from

his past crowded his mind with vivid images of rip-roaring good times and desperate midnight chases across open prairies with irate cattlemen or grim-jawed lawmen in hot pursuit . . . more often than not in the company of Sonny Boy Clanton.

Great days. Yet he'd long outgrown them by the time he'd quit to go straight and petitioned for the governor's pardon. Maybe he and Clanton had lived high and wild back then but they had certainly never kidnapped anybody, while both had regarded women as virtually sacred. Back then. . . .

Shield cleared his throat.

'Shook you up, eh, Dev? Reckoned it would. Yet somehow this dirty business doesn't seem to fit in with what you've always told me about that wild pard of yours. You painted a far better picture of him to me.'

Vallery nodded as he got to his feet. The shock was beginning to fade, cold anger replacing it.

'That is how he was, Harvey. Sonny was always real protective towards womenfolk, after what happened to his sister—'

'His sister?'

'That's a story for another time. But like I say, he was always a gentleman where ladies were concerned. Hell, he was even polite to the girls we used to meet down along the border. Treated them like real ladies, and I can tell you some were a million miles short of that.'

43

'Well, do you believe he did like everyone says?'

He had to consider before replying. Two years ago, faced with the same question, the answer would have been an unequivocal 'No!' But that was before he'd actually witnessed Sonny Boy Clanton slowly but surely begin to grow wilder and more ruthless as the posses hounded them across state borders and the spread of civilization began to intrude upon their former freedom and limit their mischief.

And he thought: the governor's daughter! It was no secret Vallery regarded that man who'd helped negotiate his freedom through amnesty as a personal friend. This also applied to Randolph's daughter whom he'd met on several occasions, enough for him to know she was pure quality.

He grimaced as he rose. This whole episode sounded more like something the Daltons would pull, or maybe Billy the Kid. But surely not the high-spirited good pard he'd once known?

'Any notion where he might have taken the girl, Dev?' the badgeman pressed.

He shook his head. 'Too many places, Harvey – too much wild country around the Panhandles, and Johnny knows every inch of it.'

Brief silence. Then, 'Dater's heading out to comb that area with his militiamen at this very moment.'

Vallery straightened sharply. He knew Colonel Nathan Dater, the chief of the territorial militia, an arrogant and dangerous man who had risen to prominence in the war against the wild men and outlaws since his militia was commissioned.

The sheriff cleared his throat. 'Do you figure Dater might catch him?'

'No chance.'

'Well, no point in holding out on you any longer, I guess. I received a wire from Governor Randolph an hour before you showed today.' He opened a drawer and produced a pink telegraph slip. 'It really concerns you.'

Vallery's confusion showed plain as he took the slip. He unfolded it with a frown, and read:

SHERIFF

HAVE EXHAUSTED ALL STEPS TO RESCUE MY DAUGHTER WITHOUT SUCCESS STOP AM IN DESPERATE NEED OF ASSISTANCE STOP REQUEST YOU CONTACT DEV STOP ASK HIM TO COME ASSIST STOP MAKE CLEAR THIS IS REQUEST NOT ORDER STOP

GOVERNOR RANDOLPH

Vallery lowered the slip to the desk top then reread it several times while the lawman studied his reaction.

'Sorry, there was no easy way of breaking this to to

you, Dev. I guess I knew how hard it would hit you. . . .' His voice trailed away.

Vallery glanced up at length, his face haggard now. 'Thanks, Harvey. And, yeah, I'll allow as how it comes as a shock.' He paused then frowned. 'But why me? I'm no manhunter or lawman—'

'I guess it's on account you likely known Sonny Boy better than any man west of the Mississippi,' the lawman said heavily. 'I guess I can understand exactly how the governor's thinking right now. You rode all that wild Panhandles country with Clanton and shared his secret trails and hideaways.' He shrugged. 'Who better qualified to help track him down and maybe find that little girl still alive than his former best pard?'

Those final words hit hard.

'Will you do it?' he was asked after a silence.

'What choice do I have?'

'Randolph insists it's a request.'

'A request from a man who I consider likely saved my life when he gave me the chance to start out fresh? No, it's more than that. I'm beholden to Governor Randolph and so I owe him.'

The chair groaned as Shields heaved his bulk erect.

'Could prove mighty dangerous if Clanton realizes you're hunting him. He'd take that mighty personal, I figure.'

Vallery didn't respond. He was envisioning what he could be letting himself in for, where it might

46

lead. He would dearly like just to head back to the spread and resume the simple life he'd created for himself there. But even had Sonny Boy not been involved in this crime the debt he owed Randolph would be enough to guarantee his involvement.

One long deep breath and the die was cast, the decision made. There was clearly no way he could not respond.

He and Sonny Boy had parted as friends. But he knew that would count for nothing when Clanton realized he was coming after him. 'If there's one stripe of polecat I hate more than any other,' he'd heard Sonny say often, 'it's a Judas. Nothing lower than a Judas . . . surely ain't. . . .'

Those words echoed in his head, yet Dev appeared calm as he turned to face the lawman. 'Don't look so down-in-the-mouth, Harvey. I'll be back.'

They shook hands wordlessly and the older man followed him as he donned his hat and stepped out onto the porch.

'You sure you've figured the risk, Dev?'

'Huh?'

'You told me once Sonny Boy was the only feller you ever met who was better with a gun than you. You didn't say you only figured that, boy, you said you knew.'

Vallery's tone was low as he replied. 'I remember, Harve.'

47

'So, are you admitting to me you could easily get yourself killed?'

Dev made no response at first, just shrugged and thrust out a hand.

'See you, Harve,' he murmured and then went swiftly down the steps. He was forced to halt as the noon stage from Greyburg came rolling by heading for the depot, billowing dust out behind and with children returning from school vacation leaning from the windows, laughing and waving.

He stood staring after the rig for a long moment, the childish voices on this calm day seeming to contrast ominously with whatever might lie ahead for him in those wilder regions of the south-west where Sonny Boy Clanton was king.

The small boy on the dusty trail looked back over his shoulder at a sudden sound and yelled, 'Look, Ma! Riders!'

The careworn woman whirled to see the dark column of oncoming horsemen then swiftly snatched up the child in her arms and toted him off the side of the trail and into a ditch.

The cavalcade hammered by with scarcely a glance, a dozen hard-faced riders in blue jackets with fading daylight glinting from cartridge belts, weapons and harness metal. The hoof-lifted dust left behind billowed sluggishly in the heat before settling slowly as the distance shrunk the horsemen to so many bobbing blobs of colour under the sun.

'Was that the militia, Ma?'

The woman's features were taut with fear and hatred as they clambered back up onto the trail. She spat in the deep dust. 'Yes, that there was Colonel Dater and his militia, son.'

'You figure they's out hunting Sonny Boy?'

'Yeah, that's just what I do reckon. . . .'

'But they won't find him, will they, Ma?'

She spat again. 'Never! Sonny Boy will always be way too smart for that pig, Dater!'

Even now in the aftermath of the crime that had turned so many former admirers of laughing Sonny Boy Clanton against him, there were those in Deaf Smith County who still refused to regard him as a genuine outlaw, just as they would never concede that many of those who hunted him were genuine heroes.

Trudging slowly back up the trail towards their shack, the woman and child didn't sight the solitary figure of the horseman outlined high upon a distant hilltop against the flaming colours of the sunset.

The rider watched them vanish into their hovel before returning his attention to the receding column of territorial militia, which he followed until it was finally swallowed up by the bare hills to the east. Only then did young Fritz Lincoln, gunman and loyal henchman of Sonny Boy Clanton, turn his horse's head and ride off towards the setting sun and the hideout in the Panhandle Mountains.

CHAPTER 4

WHERE BUZZARDS ROOST

The flames of the campfires cast huge leaping patterns across the cliff walls of the Panhandles hideout. Seated alone before his private cavern Sonny Boy Clanton lifted his head at the sound of hoofbeats. A short time later Brick Pomeroy rode into the light.

'Just got a signal from Dick down by the pass, Sonny,' the redhead called.

'Rider coming in from the east. Dick figures it's Fritz!'

'OK.'

Pomeroy immediately swung his mount around to

vanish from sight, leaving the leader to slip back into his reverie.

A short distance from Clanton's position Marlon Lord lay on his back upon folded blankets, hands locked behind his dark head as he stared up at the early stars.

Further along down by the remuda Lisa Randolph could be seen feeding sugar to the paint pony. Clanton had snatched her two days back out along the Weeping Woman River. The girl was humming to herself, her riding dress a vivid splash of crimson against the dark shapes of the horses in the pen, afraid but refusing to let it show.

The outlaws boasted many hideouts in the Panhandles wilderness but this was one of the best. The only access to their hidden valley was by a peppercorn-concealed cleft in the broad basalt rockface a half-mile below Sonny Boy's position.

The gang had never been called upon to defend the High Valley camp, but it was a certainty they'd make a murderous fight should anybody come hunting them here.

High Valley's one major disadvantage was its distance from the nearest trading post, necessitating a long haul for supplies. They were low on provisions following their return from the north. But Fritz Lincoln had set out for Fort Supply the previous night to pick up provisions and catch up on the latest news from Capital City, and was expected to return any time now.

Clanton idly plucked a blade of grass sprouting from a crack in the stones between his boots, set it between his teeth.

The man currently holding the territory to ransom appeared sober and thoughtful as he watched the girl climb the smooth rock slope leading up towards his position, openly enjoying the way she moved. She had looks and courage and a whole lot of character. Even more remarkable, however, she reminded him of his sister. . . .

He switched his attention to the campfire directly below.

Marlon Lord was also watching the girl but not in admiration. The gunman had opposed Sonny Boy's kidnap plan from the outset and nothing since had altered his attitude.

The deadly gunman believed Lisa Randolph would bring bad luck. He trusted his judgement but wasn't sure he trusted Sonny Boy's since the kidnapping.

It had been Sonny's idea alone to stage the kidnap in order to bring the governor to heel and force him to discontinue the pursuit of the gang. That had not happened and the manhunt had continued unabated. And what aggravated Lord even more was the fact that he half-suspected Lisa Randolph was wrapping Sonny around her little finger more expertly with every day.

He hadn't said as much, as yet. Even a Marlon Lord must always pick the right moment with Sonny Boy and those could prove rare at times.

So the two had avoided open conflict on the matter yet things remained strained between them as a result.

'Some sweet night, eh, Lisa?' Clanton grinned as the girl came up.

Lisa halted between the man and the fire and he watched in silence as she lowered herself to a blanket, linking hands around drawn-up knees.

'You seem very thoughtful tonight, Sonny.'

'Well, you know how it is with a rough-rider like me, Lisa,' he grinned. 'Got a lot on my mind these days.'

Her expression remained serious even when he smiled.

'I thought you might have been thinking of your sister?'

His smile faded. 'Well, now, I do get to thinking about Kate now and again I'll allow. . . .'

'You've mentioned her several times to me.'

'Guess that's on account you remind me of her some.'

'Was she really like me?'

He studied her. 'Surely was. . . .'

'Tell me about her. I know you don't care to speak of your sister, but surely it can't do any harm?'

'Maybe you're right,' he conceded after a long pause. He glanced up. 'Kate was a year older than me and really pretty. Our folks got took by the cholera when I was ten and I took care of Kate from there.'

'At just ten? Good heavens, however did you manage?'

'Looking back I often wonder. I got a job in a livery in San Antone and when things got tough, I stole. I was always kinda nippy and sneaky and never got caught. When Kate got to thirteen she took a job in a laundry. I didn't want her working but she never seemed to mind. We had a little two-room shack off a back street and got along fine, never had an argument. I reckon that was her doing, on account I was always kinda fiery but she was the opposite. . . .'

'She sounds lovely. I wish I could have met her.'

Clanton clasped his hands together tightly and a chill crept into his voice. 'You two would have hit it off just fine. But that just wasn't how it was meant to be. . . .'

'What happened to her, Sonny?'

He sucked in a deep breath.

'A drunk came to the house one night when I was working. A great big feller he was, a mule skinner. He attacked her and she fought back. He broke her neck.'

'Oh, how terrible!'

'He stole a horse and it took me five days to catch him. He was too yellow to tote a gun. I handed him one, told him to use it. Then I shot him twice in that big fat belly and sat down to watch him die. It took three hours and I wish it had been six . . . or sixty even. . . .'

He turned sharply to study her reaction and seemed to find satisfaction in the horror he saw in her face.

'I guess now you know why some folks spit and curse when they hear my name, Lisa. Well, the law got after me of course but never looked like catching me.' A pause, then, 'The law has been after me ever since but they'll never take me. Not Sonny Boy Clanton, they won't. I'll go when I'm ready, not when someone else calls time. . . .'

He broke off abruptly and jumped to his feet and turned his back, staring off into the night.

She rose to stand beside him.

'It was a terrible thing you did, Sonny. But you were only a boy . . . And your sister was all you had in the world.'

He blinked in puzzlement. She was finding excuses for him! This was exactly like Kate had done whenever he came home with a bloody nose, or maybe when someone accused him of stealing.

Emotion gripped him and he finally conceded to

himself for the first time that he felt guilty over the kidnapping, which was surely no way for any tough outlaw to operate.

And wondered if he was crazy enough to have let himself come to care for his lovely hostage. Really care. . . .

He turned to add something further when a clatter of hoofs echoed up from the trail below. Moments later Fritz Lincoln and Brick Pomeroy rode into sight and came climbing towards their position.

Marlon Lord bounced erect. 'Hey, where's them supplies?' The man whirled angrily. 'Hey, Sonny Boy, do you see what I see? Empty satchels—'

'All right, what happened?' Clanton demanded as the riders drew rein.

'Sorry, Sonny,' Lincoln drawled, slipping to ground. 'Couldn't get the stuff.'

'What do you mean – couldn't get it? You had money and you knew we were about all out. What the—'

'Dad Matthews wouldn't sell us nothing at the store, Sonny Boy,' Brick Pomeroy spoke up, pale and angry. 'Seems there are a whole mess of folks like him at Fort Supply who turned against on us on account of the kidnapping, boss.'

Lincoln cleared his throat. 'Matthews said to tell you as how he's never had nothing personal against you, Sonny. But then he went and said, "I wouldn't sell no girl-kidnapper supplies even if he was to pay me ten times over".'

A sucked-out silence fell over the outlaws' camp as Sonny Boy Clanton stared at his riders in angry disbelief.

'Why . . . that broken-winded old cowpot—' he began, but broke off sharply. Lisa was standing by his fire, listening to every word.

Lowering his voice, he drew a step closer to Pomeroy. 'Don't say any more about it,' he said softly. 'I'll square accounts soon enough and—'

'What's the matter, Sonny?' growled Marlon Lord. 'Bottling it up so your girlfriend won't get to see your mean side, pard?'

Clanton whirled. 'I've warned you about those cracks, Mar. Better put a crimp in that tongue or you just might get to regret it.'

Lord flushed but didn't respond. Nervous glances darted to and fro across the fire amongst the others. Clashes were common enough here but it was understood that whenever Clanton got riled up it was always wise to back off. All these wild young riders were dangerous, but none as lethal with the guns as the leader.

'I'll go get us those supplies,' Clanton announced finally. 'And I'll get them at Matthew's store and pay that broken-winded old cowpat off with a whippin' he'll feel until the day he croaks—'

He broke off sharply, darting a glance at Lisa Randolph. He forced a phony smile.

'So, what else?' he wanted to know. He snapped his fingers. 'C'mon – news! What's news?'

'Not good,' Lincoln sighed. 'The governor's upped the reward on you to five thousand.'

'Son of a bitch! Doesn't he know he could get himself shot doing that?'

'Well, he's proved a whole lot more stubborn than we expected,' Pomeroy pointed out. 'Now I guess he feels if he ups the ante someone close to you might be tempted to . . . well, you know. . . ?'

'I wonder if that pilgrim realizes I was in his stinking city within spitting distance of his bedchamber just the other night—' the outlaw leader began, but broke off with a quick glance at the girl. 'What about the militia?' he asked calmly. 'Any news on them blue-bellies?'

'Just like he's taken to doing most of the time lately, Dater seems to be acting independent of the governor,' the other supplied. 'We hear Randolph ordered the militia back to barracks but Dater just provisioned them up again and they're back on our scent, or at least they might think they are.'

'Grandstanding son of whore!' Lincoln hissed. 'Dater wants to oust Randolph as governor and figures if he nails us first he'd be looking good for his job. Of course if that arrogant bastard was to—'

'You're talking way too much, mister—' Clanton began, but Lincoln risked interrupting yet again.

'We did pick up something more on the militia on our way back, Sonny,' he supplied. 'Some farmers told us they seen 'em heading north.'

'But we're south—' Clanton broke off, then began to grin. 'Looking in all the wrong places, you mean?' Lincoln nodded and now the leader actually smiled broadly. 'Well, guess it ain't all bad after all.'

He folded his arms and turned sober again, brows creased in concentration.

'But something still just don't figure,' he stated as though talking to himself. 'The governor claims to want his daughter back no matter what, yet he still ain't stopping the militia hunting us. Doesn't that long-nosed son of a pious whoremonger really care whether she lives or dies?'

It would seem a fair question. They pondered it briefly before Lincoln finally spoke.

'From what I heard at Fort Supply, Sonny, Randolph don't seem to think we meant it when you said you'd finish her off if he didn't agree to make a deal with you.'

'And neither do I, Sonny.'

All swung to see that Lisa had come down the slope to halt directly behind Clanton, who turned sharply.

The girl went on. 'And he's right, isn't he, Sonny.

60

You won't kill me, will you?'

'I don't see why the hell not,' Marlon Lord put in. 'She ain't doing us one lick of good alive, Sonny, but mebbe she could do us some good dead. Maybe if we was to drill her and dump her at Capital City then Randolph would know that next time we make a play we meant business.'

Almost lazily it seemed, Sonny Boy turned and then lunged at his *segundo* to slam his fist into the side of the man's jaw with such force that Marlon Lord dropped as though pole-axed.

As the others looked on, stunned, Clanton raised his boot above Lord's face. Instantly, Lisa rushed forward to seize his arm and jerk him off balance.

'No, Sonny!' she cried. 'Please!'

Slowly the hot light faded from Clanton's eyes. He glanced down at the hand upon his sleeve, shrugged. 'All right, Lisa, OK.' He swung back on the others. 'But take a lesson, you jokers. Mar just spoke out of turn once too often. Next man that does that might get hit with a slug, not a fist.' He jerked a thumb. 'Go fetch some water!'

Lisa watched a pale Pomeroy make his way across to the water pail then tote it back to douse the contents over Lord's face. The gunfighter stirred and a thin trickle of blood ran from his mouth.

'Sonny,' Lisa said.

'Yeah?'

'Why don't you simply let me go now? For it's obvious Father realizes he can't allow you to hold the whole territory to ransom and I think you know this yourself. And I believe you'll do the fair and decent thing in the end . . . I just know it in my heart.'

Their eyes met and locked and Sonny Boy Clanton thought, who could tell? Maybe she even believed in him in the way nobody had done since Kate? And the strangest thing of all was – he suddenly wanted to be that man she thought him to be. A man with heart and compassion.

How loco was that?

Yet what if it was so?

A dazed Lord was struggling to his feet assisted by Pomeroy and Lincoln and Clanton's anger cooled.

'Finished and forgotten, Mar?' he asked quietly.

'Maybe I spoke out of turn,' Lord muttered grudgingly. 'OK, yeah . . . all finished and forgotten.'

Sonny clapped a hand to his shoulder. 'These are hard days for all of us, Mar. But they'll get better – that's a promise. All right, you saddle stiffs, start breaking camp. We're moving out.'

'Where are we going, Sonny?' Pomeroy wanted to know.

'Where else?' Clanton grinned. 'Fort Supply, of course.'

The tall man standing by the windows staring out at

the territorial flag hanging limp and motionless in the morning heat appeared to have aged years since Dev Vallery saw him last. Always lean, Governor Mitchell Randolph appeared to have shed about ten more pounds which he could not afford to lose. His well-cut grey suit hung loosely on his gaunt frame and deep hollows showed under his cheekbones, mute testimony to what the man had been put through over the past week.

'I knew you'd come, Dev,' the governor said. 'And I feel badly, having had to ask you. When you told me once you'd do anything to repay me for granting you amnesty I never dreamed I'd have to call upon you to make good on that promise. Certainly never under such circumstances.'

'I guess I'd have ended up coming down whether you asked or not, Governor,' Vallery replied, and meant every word. The governor's plea had simply brought him here a little quicker, was all.

Randolph's eyes showed his gratitude as he returned to the wall map of Deaf Smith County and they studied it together at some length. 'An immense area, Dev. One hell of a big country in which to hide one small girl.'

'But not big enough to hide Sonny Boy from me, Governor. If he's still in this territory, I'll find him.'

'You know, I believe you will. So, where do you propose to begin?'

'The Panhandles. '

'You'll need men, of course. I still have some militiamen available here at the mansion for—'

'No, not militiamen.'

'You still don't trust our special troopers, Dev?'

'It's not the men I mistrust. It's Colonel Dater.'

Randolph sighed.

'An almost universal attitude, I fear. Very well, your objection is duly noted. I shall set about finding others to ride with you.'

'There are several men working here in Capital City who took amnesty with me, Governor. Hardcases, no doubt, but good gunhands and fighters. I reckon I'll need their kind of backing before this is over.'

'Excellent suggestion. My clerk has a list of all amnestees. I'll set him to rounding up those who you need immediately, Dev. And while he's so engaged you and I shall take lunch.'

Dev was feeling reinvigorated when they went down to the main courtyard an hour later to meet the men the governor's people had assembled for him. He knew them all – former wild ones and just plain hardcases who'd taken amnesty as he had done, with quite a number actually working with the authorities now.

Vallery greeted the men and explained the purpose of their mission while the governor issued special rations from the supply stores. Each man was provided with ammunition and a deputy's star for the duration of the search. They would be paid five dollars per day while out on the trail, with the added incentive of sharing in the major reward should they take Sonny Boy Clanton either dead or alive.

'I guess your name still carries a lot of weight around here, Dev,' Randolph commented as the squad made ready to leave. 'None of these men would ride with Dater yet all jumped at the chance of joining you.'

'Well, all I can say is I hope they aren't proven wrong.'

'They aren't.' Randolph was emphatic. He shook his hand. 'You can do it . . . and you will, won't you, Dev? You'll bring my little girl back to me. . . .'

'Governor, have no doubts. I'll bring Lisa back safe and sound.'

They rode out in brilliant sunshine, striking due south from Capital City across the heat-baked plains. Unease and uncertainty had been Dev Vallery's companions on the ride down from the north, but he was free of both now.

And doubted that even the governor would ever suspect that, ever since the early days when he'd first met Lisa Randolph here at the capital, he believed he'd been in love with her.

He still felt that way, but knew it was impossible, of

course. Well-bred young women of position and breeding never fell for gunmen-hellions even if they reformed a dozen times over.

That was reality and he accepted it.

He rode easily in the saddle as the swift miles fell behind, passing old familiar landmarks to reach at length the beginning of the broken country where the lofty stone teeth of the Panhandles chopped like fish teeth into a bleached blue sky.

His expression grew grim and his lips moved.

'I never figured it would ever come to this, Sonny Boy,' he murmured. 'Now it's you or me, old partner . . . just you or me. . . .'

CHAPTER 5

BADMAN OR HERO?

Darkness fell on Victory and oil lamps flared and flickered eerily along the full length of the crooked main stem. The muggy breeze that came with the night brought little relief from the long day's heat.

The desert outpost situated close to the remote eastern border of Deaf Smith County was small, poor and ugly, comprising a sparse scattering of unpainted shacks and hovels surrounding the hotel, saloon, store, blacksmith shop and rickety post office. There were towns in other sectors of the region now where progress was vigorously on the march, but Victory had been born a backwater cowtown ten years earlier and had been slowly sliding backwards ever since.

Colonel Dater's expression revealed exactly what he thought of Victory as he led his blue-jacketed troopers down the dusty main street just on eight. The chief of territorial militia was hot and sweaty in his heavy serge coat and his manner was testy as he barked orders at his men while dismounting before the Cowboy Saloon.

Flexing aching back muscles and ignoring a scatter of gaping porch loafers, he paused momentarily to sweep the street with a suspicious look before shouldering his way through the batwing doors of the town's only watering hole.

'Whiskey!' he barked, then took a chair and surveyed the room.

The whiskey was cloudy and tasted so rough it brought tears to his eyes. Yet it cleared the trail dust from his throat and immediately began lifting his fatigue.

'Is he here?' he barked to nobody in particular.

'No, Colonel,' a drinker nervously replied. Everyone knew who he meant.

'Has he been here?'

'Not in many weeks, Colonel,' Oaks answered from behind the bar.

'And you wouldn't tell me even if he had, would you, you fly-blown misfit?'

The question did not call for a reply and the bartender offered none. He made a pretence of cleaning glasses as Dater poured himself another jolt of rye.

The chief of the territorial militia was a big man with a hard fleshy face and heavy shoulders. He was overweight yet moved quickly and with purpose. He had spent ten years in army forts along the North-west Frontier before coming to South-west Territory. Prior to the appointment of Mitchell Randolph as governor there were rumours that the region might be placed under martial law with Dater promoted to general in command. Many believed this could still happen should Randolph fail to bring true law and order to the territory, in particular Deaf Smith County.

Dater had worked his way through three glasses of the rough whiskey before his sergeant returned.

'Well?' he growled.

The report wasn't encouraging. Nobody had sighted his quarry but his men seemed to believe many here had turned against Sonny Boy since the abduction.

'I'll believe that when I see it. Mail?'

Cole tugged an envelope from his jacket. 'Letter from the governor, sir. Postmaster says it came in yesterday.'

Dater ripped the envelope open and scanned the contents. His face darkened.

'Anything wrong, Colonel?'

'That damned fool! He's sent Vallery out to search independently. Says if we make contact with Clanton

I'm to offer any assistance Vallery might require!'

The sergeant's brows lifted sharply. 'Would that be Dev Vallery, Colonel?'

'How many Vallerys do you know, mister?'

'But . . . but last I heard Vallery had quit the territory and the game. Nobody's seen or heard anything of him since he took amnesty.'

'Well, he's heard of now.' Dater's mouth twisted viciously. 'Go lose yourself, damnit! I've got some thinking to do about this.'

But thinking didn't come easy, and Dater finally realized what he really needed was a hot tub and some peace and quiet. Within minutes he was up to his thick neck in soapsuds in the bath-house in back of the Territory Hotel.

He swirled water lazily over his barrel chest and felt the weariness ease out of him as he reviewed his situation.

His assignment to run down Sonny Boy Clanton might appear straightforward to some, yet looked far from that to the eye of Colonel Dater. For he believed that if Clanton's reign were to continue it would eventually lead to the governor's dismissal and martial law introduced to replace his administration.

Martial law here simply meant Colonel Nathan Dater. He would be promoted to general in command and saw no limit to how far that might take him, should it come to pass.

And all this hinged upon one dirty little killer who was still shy of his twenty-third birthday!

Then his thoughts switched to Vallery and gloom descended again. For if Vallery succeeded where he had publicly failed, where might that leave him?

He dressed quickly and hurried off to find the woman he always looked up whenever he stopped off at Victory.

Blue-eyed Vera acted pleased to see him and next morning found the colonel brimming with purpose as he appeared on the streets ready to lead his squad from town.

Good news awaited him. His top sergeant had overnight come by fresh intelligence on their quarry. There had been a sighting of Clanton far from Victory in the south Panhandles some twenty miles north-west of Fort Supply just two days earlier.

Dater's eyes glinted. 'Fort Supply! We know the scum shows up there every so often . . .' He stroked his hard jaw. 'Very well, Coe, it sounds as if this tip-off might well be genuine. We'll find out.'

They made a brave sight riding out two abreast with the banner of the territorial militia fluttering above their heads, but nobody cheered. Folks in Victory didn't hold themselves high, but even the bums and three-time losers on these mean streets rated themselves better than Colonel Dater.

*

Dev Vallery halted atop the crest of the cottonwood slope and his men reined in behind. Squinting into the glare of the morning sun he drew his shirt sleeve across his sweating face. Red Feather Mesa was a shimmering blob of colour far to the east. To the west, twisting its tortuous route through the dry foothills of the rugged middle sector of the Panhandles, tiny Silver Creek shimmered in the light.

He swallowed a swig from his canteen then led the way onwards into the mounting heat, occasionally halting to study old tracks. So far old sign was the only kind to be seen. But he would persist for this was a remote yet familiar region which he and Clanton had ridden often together in the past.

Long horse miles fell behind in dreary monotony until he halted the squad and swung down, the others following suit. Instructing the men to stay put, he scouted ahead with his Winchester to follow the course of a shallow ravine for a mile before clambering out at the point where an ancient landslide blocked it off.

Familiar territory.

The old bunch had made their way back into the Panhandles from this direction often in the old days. A mile south they'd buried Joey Winslow when he stopped the slug that mattered most in a skirmish with bounty hunters back at Firebrush Ravine.

The valley seemed empty of life.

Shouldering the rifle he worked his way downhill into the valley itself to inspect a series of old and blackened campfire sites, later squatted in the shade of a peppercorn tree to build a cigarette and do some thinking on places they'd visited with familiar names such as Choctaw Gap, Reedy Creek, High Valley. . . .

High Valley!

Vallery uncoiled to his feet and flicked the half-smoked cigarette away. High Valley was as remote as Dead Squaw but had the added advantage of being a natural defensive position. It could well be that factor which might attract Sonny Boy's thinking right now.

The clatter of his boot-heels echoed against rock walls as he quit the basin and climbed back to the peppercorn crest. He squinted at the sun for a minute before heading downslope for the ravine. It was just past noon. He reckoned that by taking the old miners' trail through Jim Dandy Canyon they should make High Valley around midnight.

The moment he entered the room Sonny Boy Clanton felt the tension.

He paused momentarily with eyes flicking from one sober face to another before crossing to the rough bar to slap the plank top for service.

The whiskey was good but two big swallows didn't improve his mood.

'So?' he growled at Lord, who was smartest of the bunch – smart and tetchy. The man was good at most everything, including the ability to rub Clanton up the wrong way.

'It ain't working, is what,' the man said at last.

'What ain't?' Clanton's tone was flat.

'The damned woman is what. We been discussing and agree that while snatching her was supposed to force Randolph to ease up on us, instead, it's worked just the opposite. There's bluecoats every place a man looks these days and—'

'What are you driving at?'

'We reckon if this goes on much longer we could all wind up on Randolph's gibbet at Capital City. So we figure if he wants his damned daughter we just hand her back. Right, boys?'

Heads bobbed. Clanton showed surprise. 'OK, boys, if that's how you feel—'

'In a box!'

Lord's words silenced him. Clanton stared, the colour draining from his face. 'What?'

Lord's hands were on lean hips, eyes hard. 'If she went back alive there'd be no reason for Randolph to quit on us. But if she's dead – there won't be any reason for him to keep after us, don't you see? It would be too damn late!'

His gaze flicking from man to man, Clanton realized this had been building up and what he was confronting bordered on rebellion.

Anger grabbed him but he didn't let it show. Should he brace them all he could easily wind up dead. For unlike himself, some were killers, while Lord was likely as fast with a gun as himself.

'OK, OK,' he said, impressively calm. 'Give me time to consider. Could take a couple of hours.'

They were suspicious, yet at the same time relieved.

As expected, it was Marlon Lord who made the decision.

'OK, a couple hours. We'll meet back here at midnight.'

'Right.' Clanton started for the door, then swung back and tossed a bill onto the plank bar. 'For my pards,' he told the woman. He tossed them a final salute, amazed he could fake a smile when his anger was raging. 'See you then.'

Nobody answered. None had expected him simply to walk away. It seemed out of character. It was.

Sonny Boy Clanton stood beside Lisa Randolph's horse next day. His hat hung down his back by the throat strap as he chewed on a blade of grass and watched the tiny figures moving about the way station of the Butterfield Stage Line far below.

'They're getting ready for the four o'clock stage

coming in from Trinidad down there, Lisa,' Clanton stated quietly, gesturing at the way station and the winding ribbon of trail. 'You'll make it down there easy. You should be back in Capital City by ten tomorrow.'

'I-I don't quite know what to say, Sonny . . . except thank you.'

'Forget it, Lisa, you sure don't have nothing to thank me for, considering what I did to you. But you never know. Maybe you might just be able to do me a good turn someday? Who knows?'

The girl studied his unlined face. More than once she'd feared she might die out here in the wilds but now it seemed sure she was being handed her life back.

'I've been thinking about the future ever since you decided to send me back home, Sonny. My father is going to be eternally grateful to you for this. And he always listens to me, so surely there must be something I could do for you. I know the amnesty offer is closed, yet I'm sure I could persuade father to make an exception in your case and—'

He laughed softly.

'That ain't my way, Lisa. Soon as I gave up my guns every man with a grudge and a gun would come calling and next thing I'd find myself lying under a headstone. That quick.'

'But others have done it.'

76

'But not Sonny Boy Clanton.' He smiled up at her. 'Forget it, girl. I'll just play out the hand I've been dealt. Too late for me to change now.'

'You mustn't say that. You could change, I know it.'

The outlaw turned sober, realizing she really didn't understand. For violence had tainted his life and was a deep-rooted part of him. How could a girl like this ever understand that. And yet it was important to him that she go on regarding him as just some unlucky kid the world had pushed around, which despite his notoriety was largely how he saw himself.

She must go now . . . and never know he had fallen in love with her.

'You'd best be riding,' he said with an air of finality. 'That old stage is going to come bowling along any time now.'

He saw the bright glitter of tears in her eyes, then she leaned quickly from the saddle and kissed him on the mouth.

'Goodbye, Sonny Boy,' she whispered. 'Go with God.'

She was swiftly gone, loping down the long dry grass slope on the paint pony he'd stolen for her along Weeping Woman River. Her hair streamed in the wind and reminded him of liquid gold. She did not look back and he was glad of it.

He turned slowly and his walk appeared strangely stiff as he made his slow way back to his horse. He suddenly felt like the oldest man in the territory.

'So, that's what you went and done, eh, Sonny?' Dick Rutherford's voice was carefully controlled.

Sonny Boy stood with hands on hips. 'Yeah, I done it right enough.'

Silence. He had kept their appointment back at the rickety old plank bar, strolling in casually to report that by then the governor's daughter would be within a couple of hours' travel time from Capital City.

He'd returned ready for anything. Reconciliation. Rage. Rebellion. Maybe even gunplay. . . ?

Gunplay could have been possible. For the gang's old closeness was not what it had been. While the Lord faction grew wilder and more ruthless, Sonny Boy often appeared to be drifting . . . having a good time when he could and still very much top man – but different.

Yet nothing happened.

He'd deliberately played a high-risk card and all knew it. But these men weren't fools. Sure, they could easily gang up on him. But for what purpose now? The governor's daughter was gone. Were they willing to risk bracing him for no gain?

He looked a question at Marlon Lord until at length the tall gunman shrugged, slapped his chest with both hands and turned back to the bar.

'Set 'em up, Rosie,' he growled. 'Five shots . . . on me.'

Sonny Boy sighed in relief. He'd been ready for most anything but plainly the crisis was at an end. He knew he'd lost standing over the matter but knew he could reclaim it. If he wanted. . . .

But for now he was content to drink down the moon . . . and try not think about the governor's daughter.

Daylight saw him saunter from the bar to fit boot to stirrup and swing up into his saddle. Still without a word he started off and didn't look back. The others were being put to a test. After an uncertain minute the four traded glances, shrugged then legged it out to their mounts and rode after him.

Sonny Boy might have slipped some off his pedestal but was still number one in this outfit.

CHAPTER 6

HELLER WITH
A SIXGUN

Macsmith had always been a hard man and appeared to have toughened up even more since they'd last met. Gambler, standover man, former jailbird and knife artist, he was not somebody to approach casually even if your name did happen to be the one which was on everybody's lips in Capital City that day.

Dev Vallery was back in the city and was visiting the High Ace Saloon. Yet Macsmith managed to appear unimpressed as the one-time hellraiser turned cattle rancher shouldered his way through the swinging doors and crossed directly to him where he was lounging against the long bar, pint of beer in fist.

'Straighten up, Macsmith, I want to talk to you.'

Macsmith scowled and flexed big pectoral muscles beneath his cheap shirt as he straightened to full height. He was taller than Vallery and fifty pounds heavier, all of it solid muscle.

'Let me guess.' His voice sounded like a bumble-bee in a gourd. 'You're Randolph's hot-shot what's come down to try and chase Sonny Boy up a tree. Right?'

'That's me. And you're the loser they tell me feeds Sonny inside information on jobs he might pull or herds to raid? Right?'

Macsmith was a pro. He revealed no hint of intent before he lashed out with a hairy fist. He found noth-ing but air as Vallery bobbed low, then came up behind a brutal right hook to the jaw that had every ounce of his one-eighty pounds behind it.

Macsmith blinked. He thought Dev was loco. When Macsmith realized he was deadly serious, the bruiser turned brick-red and threw a powerhouse right for the jaw.

The blow never landed but Vallery's brutal left hook to the point saw the heavyweight stagger back yards before he struck the bar and fell forward on his face.

It took five minutes to bring Macsmith around by which time he had stopped bleeding from the mouth and was ready to sing like a bird.

'F-Fort Supply,' he managed to croak with twenty

wide-eyed drinkers and derelicts looking on. 'Er, j-just a chance the bunch could be headin' there . . . er, Mr Vallery . . . sir.'

Vallery turned to face the room. 'Anyone else got anything to say?'

There were no takers. With a nod to the saloon-keeper he walked out onto the street where the sun shone bright on Capital City.

Only now did he pause to suck skinned knuckles. He'd enjoyed that, even if Macsmith did have a jaw of cement. He adjusted his hat and headed directly for the palace.

He'd genuinely wanted information but the incident behind him had also been intended to remind the city just who he was and what he was about. In his wilder days he'd learned the best way to impress some folks was to go in hard from the start. This scared some but with others it could have the effect of loosening their tongues and encouraging them to confide information, usually in the hope of reward.

He was aware of the stir he was creating as he strode across the Plaza of Heroes. Indeed, the capital had been buzzing with excitement ever since the governor's daughter had been returned unharmed. And by Sonny Boy Clanton personally, or so everybody now believed.

Naturally, Vallery was vastly relieved to learn that Lisa Randolph was back at the governor's palace, and was at that very moment breakfasting with her father.

The Randolphs and others were ready to attribute Sonny Boy's astonishing back-flip to Dev's presence but he wasn't buying that. He knew Sonny that well. There was some other reason behind his actions which he might learn in time.

But what he believed by this was that Sonny was still the major ongoing threat down here. Yet opinions on his former pard seemed mixed, although the kidnapping had shown that Clanton was now ready to dare anything or take any risk, whereas in the old days most of the stunts he had pulled seemed half in fun.

Yet the man who'd abducted the governor's daughter had then returned her, which sounded just like the quirky man he'd known. But now, as always, he was keenly aware of Sonny's cleverness, quick brain and total fearlessnes, and was realizing that, despite the unexpected outcome of the kidnapping, he might have no option but to stay on here in the south until Sonny was brought to justice. He reckoned he might be the only man who could do it.

The storekeeper at remote and lawless Fort Supply was by nature a sober and cautious citizen who nonetheless had taken angry exception to Sonny Boy Clanton's abduction of the governor's daughter. Considering the fact that the manhunt for Clanton and his hostage had increased dramatically over recent days, certainly nobody out along the Southwest Trail expected that heller to show up in their town, particularly now that both the militia and Colonel Dater were also fully involved in the manhunt.

Added to this was the fact that the governor now had enough reward money riding on Clanton's scalp to make almost any public place seem far too dangerous for the outlaw leader to risk visiting these days.

Dad Matthews would not be the first man to figure wrong about Sonny Boy. Lawmen, bounty hunters and the troopers of Deaf Smith County had been making such errors for years. Yet even though Matthews had been around long enough to understand what Clanton could be like if crossed, he'd still allowed outrage to cloud his wiser judgement when he'd refused to sell Fritz Lincoln provisions last time the man came calling.

The storekeeper wouldn't realize his error until too late.

It was late evening. There was but a handful of customers in the battered old general store when they heard the clatter of horses drawing up outside. A large and fearsome man with black hair and broad shoulders, Dad Matthews was drawing sorghum from a barrel for Widow James when the musical jingle of spurs heralded the arrival of more customers.

The storekeeper glanced up, froze. Widow James turned her head and went pale with one hand clapped to her heart. A cracker-barrel loafer started for the doors, thought better of it and simply froze as though rooted to the spot, staring.

The only one beneath the old iron roof who appeared relaxed and brimming with good cheer was the slim young man with the smiling blue eyes who strolled in to make his leisurely way across to the long counter.

'How about a little good, old-fashioned service, Dad, old pard?' Clanton drawled, slapping the counter with the flat of his hand.

Dad Matthews seemed riveted to the spot as customers turned sharply to see Marlon Lord follow his leader through the doorway, to be trailed in turn by Rutherford, Lincoln and Pomeroy.

The entire Clanton gang!

All the wild boys were grinning and this seemed the scariest thing of all. When Clanton spoke again his voice was filled with mock concern.

'What's ailing you, Dad? You ain't looking good at all. Hey boys, don't you think old Pop is looking real poorly tonight?'

'Powerful poorly, Sonny Boy,' Dick Rutherford agreed. 'Wonder if it's something he ate ... or mebbe do you figure it could be something he done?'

Somehow the storekeeper found his voice. 'Now, Sonny Boy, you got no call to be mad at me. I only done what any man rightly would—'

'Me, mad?' Clanton sounded astonished. He moved along the counter, hands spread wide. 'Why should I be mad? I mean, any storekeeper's got the right to choose his customers, I always say. Nobody says he's got to serve just any bum who might sashay through his doors, now do they?'

Cold sweat sheened Matthews's features. He was the biggest man in town yet was shaking in his boots.

'Sonny Boy, you shouldn't be here. They're hunting you all over and—'

He broke off with a gasp as Clanton reached across the counter with lightning speed to clutch his leather apron, two-handed. With an incredible show of strength he hauled the heavy man off his feet and clear across his counter to nose-dive him deliberately into the floor at his feet. Gasping, bleeding and half-conscious, Matthews made to rise but a small Star boot slammed down hard on his chest, pinning him there.

Clanton wasn't smiling any longer. 'I always treated you real good, Dad,' he panted. 'Yet you turned against me like a yeller dog. You just shouldn't have done that, Dad . . . on account I surely never could abide a stinking Judas—'

He broke off abruptly. The big man was blubbering and holding up shaking hands like a child. 'Please, Sonny, please. . . .'

Clanton appeared stunned. He'd regarded this man as a force of nature, as did everybody.

'Give him a good kicking, Sonny!'

It was Lord who spoke. But it was already all over. Showing the mercurial temperament that many knew so well, Clanton bent swiftly, hauled the shuddering big man to his feet, patted him on the top of his head and in the next instant was was smiling beatifically and leaning lazily upon the counter top.

Twinkling blue eyes held the onlookers in place as though hypnotised. 'Nobody's ever too old to learn a lesson, eh, folks?'

None of the men responded. Only the diminutive Widow Jones had the nerve to step forward.

'You're bad, Sonny Boy Clanton!' she shrilled. 'I was never sure of it before but you are surely just plain bad to the bone!'

The outlaw's smile broadened.

'Too true, Ma'am, just too damned true – if you'll excuse my language.'

'Standing there grinning like a jackass after half killing poor Mr Matthews!' Once started, the woman seemed unable to stop. 'Well, you'll be laughing on the other side of your wicked face soon! Just wait until Dev Vallery catches up with you. You won't be laughing any—'

'Hey, slow right down there, ma'am!' Clanton frowned. 'What's this about my old pal, Dev?'

The widow gaped. 'You don't know?'

'Don't know what?'

She smiled triumphantly. 'Why, he's come hunting for you is what, Mister Know Nothing! Yes, it's true and you didn't even know it. My glory but isn't that rich!'

Clanton was incredulous. 'Why . . . why, that's a dirty lie, you old crow! Dev and me go all the way back. He wouldn't—'

'What she says is so, Sonny,' weighed in a customer. 'The news reached here just today. Vallery and a bunch of amnestees rode out of Capital City yesterday and the governor's got him spearheading the big hunt for you and his daughter, we're told.'

Clanton still appeared shocked. For in his rare reflective moments he'd always believed he'd made but the one genuine friend in his life, and that was Vallery. Yet now they expected him to believe the same pard was out hunting for him along with the rest of Randolph's running dogs!

'Not true,' he muttered, and glared from face to face as though daring them to argue until the counterman nervously produced a copy of the current issue of the *Capital City Sentinel* and placed it upon the counter top.

And there it was for all to see.

The headlines fully covering Vallery's return to Capital City for a conference with the governor, resulting in the former wild man officially joining the hunt for Sonny Boy Clanton, were penned in jubilant style. It seemed plain that the editor at least considered the manhunt a foregone success despite the failures of a dozen posses which had been searching for the outlaw and his hostage across half the county.

Clanton's face was bloodless as he finally flung the paper aside.

He strode past a still-shaking prostrate Matthews and shouldered his way blindly out through the swinging doors to jump astride his horse at the tie-rack and stormed off down the short length of the street before swinging off onto the trail to Paradise.

Paradise lay ten miles west and was the nearest place where a man could buy a real drink.

'Reckon the man's got the right idea,' Marlon Lord remarked as the quartet stepped out onto the front gallery. 'Hell, after this bit of news I reckon we all need a shot!'

'Damn right,' agreed Lincoln. But then he hunkered down calmly and deliberately took out the makings. 'But let's give him plenty time to cool down. I ain't seen Sonny this sore since . . . well, since ever, I wouldn't be surprised.'

That seemed a sensible idea to men who'd never

seen wild Sonny looking anything like this shocked – and mad.

As Governor Mitchell Randolph had remarked to his troopers in the courtyard of the palace at Capital City the previous day, the name of fast Dev Vallery still could raise emotions and reactions around Deaf Smith County.

'Having another, Sonny Boy?' asked the bartender.

'Go straight to hell!'

The man behind the bar paled. 'Hell, sorry, Sonny, I just figgered—'

'No, damnit, it's me that should be sorry, Jack,' Clanton said, forcing a grin. He spun a gold coin upon the bar. 'Here, have a shot. Hell, pour everybody a shot. . . .'

He glanced up as the stranger came in through the batwings, a tall gaunt man in a weather-tained coat who walked with a limp.

'Who are you?' he challenged.

The bounty hunter gulped and froze. 'Er—'

'Who cares anyway?' Clanton snapped, and turned his back. He was in that kind of a mood, amiable one moment and acting scary and dangerous the next. Drinkers gave him plenty room as he returned to the bar, allowing the stranger in the long coat to move further along, where he ordered himself a double.

'Have another, Sonny?' Lord said.

'Why not?' Clanton shoved his glass across the bar. He studied his image in the mirror and saw how pale he looked. Pale and still mad. 'It's hard to believe, Mar.' He gestured violently. 'Riding for Randolph! What the—'

'Take it easy, man. Just one gun ain't going to make that much difference.'

'You're wrong! If it's Dev's gun it will make plenty difference.'

'You know, looking back, I guess it wasn't such a great idea after all, pard.'

Clanton turned to stare at the man. 'What?'

Lord gestured. 'Grabbing that dame. Sure, for a spell Randolph held off us some, but now he's got her back he's got half the freaking county out hunting us and—'

'Shut up!'

Lord looked offended. 'Hey, take it easy, man. I was only saying what I—'

He broke off as Clanton grabbed his arm and stared up at the bar mirror, every muscle suddenly tense.

'What is it, Sonny?'

'Shut up! Everybody shut up.' The outlaw was turning slowly, setting his glass aside, his head tilting in a listening attitude. 'Something ain't right. . . .'

Sonny Boy Clanton had always possessed an uncommon instinct for self-preservation. At that moment it suddenly seemed there was too much noise in this room . . . or maybe not enough? Whatever, it was sufficient to cause him to close his right hand over the walnut Colt handle as he swung about to sweep his gaze around the bar-room, every instinct clamouring now.

And sighted the tall gaunt man in a shabby weather-coat at the far end of the room furtively drawing a concealed six-hooter!

Clanton dropped belly-flat faster than the eye could follow and drew in the same instant.

The bounty man's shot crashed deafeningly loud and the bullet creased the diving outlaw's curved back, just behind the right shoulder. Instantly Marlon Lord's lightning Colt leapt and roared and Sim Ollinger was smashed back dead with a bullet through the heart.

Before the bounty man hit the floor five more bullets had ripped into his body.

In the sucked-out silence that followed only Sonny Boy seemed unaffected by it all despite the fact he'd plainly been the gunman's target.

He didn't even check his bullet crease as Lord stood beside him wreathed in gunsmoke and feeding fresh shells into his piece from his belt.

The rest in the room seemed momentarily frozen.

'Who is he?' His tone was level, his manner calm.

A red-nosed loser sleeved cold sweat from his face.

'Name's Ollinger, Sonny. Bounty hunter. Guess I was the only one who recognized him when he come to town. He told me not to say nothin' or he'd put me in the ground.'

Clanton went to the bar. 'Double rye,' he said. Then, 'Get him out of here.'

It was hushed for a time after the corpse was removed and the swamper grabbed up a mop to clean away the bloodstains. The outlaws tried to appear nonchalant but didn't quite succeed.

Marlon Lord lighted a cheroot and drew deep. He was also wary now.

'Reckon we ought to be dusting, Sonny.'

'Why?'

'Well . . . we been here long enough, ain't we?'

'Mebbe.' Sonny looked at the tall gunman. 'Good work, Mar. One I owe you.'

He paused and gazed around. 'First Dev . . . now this sonova!' Then his trade-mark smile reappeared. 'I must be getting more important than I figured.'

Sonny Boy leaned his back against an upright.

'You know, it seems to me that folks have been coming down with the wrong notions about me of late. Tenth-raters try to do me in – storekeepers acting uppity. And now – old pards turning Judas on me, by God!'

Marlon Lord knew Clanton better than the others. He'd admired him hugely once but that was diminishing by the day. Clanton was the best guntipper he'd ever seen but seemed to be changing a little every day. His abduction of the governor's daughter had been daring and brilliant, yet had failed in its purpose, while in the eyes of many, Lord included, he'd lost status in returning her to her family unharmed and with nothing gained.

And now – a dirty bounty hunter almost getting the jump on him was like a further assault on his pride and status. Lord felt he should do something quick to show the world that Sonny Boy was in reality bigger and bolder than ever to reclaim lost status.

Lord cleared his throat. 'So, what next?'

'I will see both Randolph and Dater dead inside the month,' Clanton promised. 'But a Judas rates high above even those bastards – way above, in truth. So my Judas ex-pard will first—'

He swung to face the room and raised his voice. 'You can all hear this so you can spread the word. I'm gonna kill Vallery and he won't have any trouble finding me. If he don't have the guts to come here for me the whole Territory will know it. Then I'll go after him but he won't even know it before he's dead!'

Marlon Lord absorbed the room's reaction. He shrugged. When Clanton spoke this way it was difficult to doubt him.

But Lord realized *he* was doubting, and some time

later as he sat drinking with the others, the gunman did some heavy thinking. More than ever he reckoned Sonny wasn't the man he'd once been – that some change or maybe even softness had overtaken him. Which meant that sooner or later Marlon Lord might have to make his move.

Challenge the leader?

Lord felt a shiver pass over his lean body at the thought. He was ambitious and regarded himself as Clanton's equal with a .45 – yet was aware that the very notion of challenging fast Sonny Boy seemed to turn his blood to water. Sonny Boy had won every gunfight he'd ever been in and likely always would.

He wondered if this was something Dev Vallery might have forgotten.

CHAPTER 7

THE GODLESS BREED

Dawn light was beginning to stain the sky as the riders clattered down through the dry hills north-west of Shafter's Station on the Butterfield Stage Line. They kept to a steady pace, conserving horse stamina with Dev Vallery leading the way. Before them in the dust lay the fading hoof prints they'd picked up several miles from the deserted outlaw camp up at High Valley. The manhunters had been forced to rest up during the hours of darkness between moonset and first light and were now pushing hard to make up for lost time.

Vallery had finally committed himself to a full-scale manhunt for the outlaws following Lisa's

96

release. He saw it as both unexpected and heartening that Sonny had returned the girl safe and sound . . . but had anything really changed?

For the gang was still very much at large with Sonny posing an even greater threat than he'd been before. Vallery regarded the fact that Clanton had been able to strike right at the very heart of territory security with the kidnapping as proof positive he was now more ruthlessly capable than ever.

Vallery had wanted to head for home but knew now he would not be doing that. As a former pard of Sonny Boy he felt a responsibility to the entire area to see this through now, and would.

Two miles on saw him rein up and swing down a little stiffly to study the tracks they believed might belong to the gang.

'Where do you figure they're making for, Dev?' Bob Beckwith was a lean man, good with horses. 'Ain't nothing much away out this way. You reckon maybe this is just a blind? That he might be tricking us into thinking they're going one way when they're planning to cut back and maybe be heading in another?'

'Could be. . . .'

Vallery moved away, pacing up and down the sign and massaging his jaw. He halted and stood off in the direction the sign was pointing, due east. He knew this desolate country backwards. East of this remote region lay nothing but more of the same – lifeless canyon country, bleak and empty landscapes and ever-diminishing water and game.

And the escarpment!

He realized now he'd overlooked this fifty-mile long and thousand-feet high natural barricade in terms of an escape route. Mile High Escarpment, not even visible from where he stood now, had long been regarded as an impossible barricade between the plains and the high rolling lands of the Divide beyond.

Yet there was a trail.

It was so long back since he had climbed that ancient Comanche track with a posse at his heels, he'd virtually forgotten it until now.

Maybe that was where the gang was heading . . . if indeed these were their tracks? He'd reckoned Sonny had been acting out of character ever since the incident at Capital City and that, just at the moment, he could be more interested in avoiding trouble than creating it.

He based this on the simple fact that they'd not been ambushed yet. That wasn't like the Sonny he knew. So, if his quarry was bent on avoiding further trouble, then that old escarpment route could be on his mind. But surely this was too long and challenging a journey to decide on quickly?

He reached a decision.

'We'll ride on down to Shafter's Station and find out if they passed through there. It won't cost us much time and it just might stop us maybe making a big mistake.'

The sun was lifting clear of the hills as they sighted their objective. Smoke curled lazily from the station chimney and they could see a man out back pitching hay into the horse corrals. As they hit level going and drummed on towards the cluster of buildings two figures appeared on the long front gallery to watch them come in. Dev immediately recognized a face from the old days. Chad Shafter was the station boss.

'Howdy, Chad!' he called as they reined in and stepped down.

He drew no response. Shafter merely stared down at him, hard-faced. Dev was hardly surprised. Two years ago at this very place he and Sonny Boy had 'playfully' held guns on this man while the rest of the bunch hunted around for something to eat and not pay for.

He put on an easy smile as he mounted the steps. 'Relax, Chad. I'm riding the opposite side of the fence these days.'

'So I hear.' Shafter ran his eyes over Vallery's uniformed companions, then grunted. 'So, what brings you out this way?'

They told him, and the station boss shook his

head. 'No sign of them cutting this way.' He studied Dev thoughtfully. 'Seems curious you hunting Sonny Boy Clanton. You two were always good buddies.'

Dev just nodded but said nothing. He didn't want to remember the good days. A man needed a clear head and no baggage from the past to succeed at a job like this.

The party sat down to coffee and conversation and it soon became clear to Vallery that what information the depot was able to supply wasn't strong enough to warrant riding further.

Dev sampled his joe and it was good. After a brief silence he glanced at each man in turn and delivered his bombshell. 'Well, if everybody's rested up we'll saddle up and get going.'

Everybody stared. Then all began talking at once. They had sign to follow, they protested. Good sign.

But Vallery just shook his head.

'Bad sign,' he corrected. 'Sonny and I used to lay false trails like this back in the old days. This looks like that same old trick to me.'

'You mean we're really quitting on Clanton, Dev?' Beckwith asked aggrievedly.

'We'll never quit,' Vallery cut him off. 'Just playing it smart, is all. Let's ride.'

And ride they did. Some were angry and others relieved. Yet each man kept his silence as he swung up and headed for the trail. Dev led the way and invited no further comment on his decision. He, too, was disappointed for he'd made a solemn vow to capture Sonny Boy or bust himself trying.

But he refused to gamble on uncertainties. He couldn't envision Clanton tackling that Mile High track. What he was now planning to do was muster a real posse, wait until the outlaws made their next mistake, then go after them with everything they had and stay on the trail until their quarry were either dead or in chains.

He was playing this game for keeps and sensed Sonny would do the same. And yet it was easy enough even for Dev Vallery to overlook the fact that when pressed, Sonny Boy might simply pour himself a shot and scratch his curly head himself.

Clanton was feeling better with every horse mile that carried him steadily closer to his objective, and knew his decision would pan out to be right.

Right and crazy, maybe. But didn't they say love could make a man loco at times?

The horse was moving easily beneath him as the sun slid down to the western rim and the high watch towers and brooding mud-brick walls of Capital City loomed directly ahead. For what more did a man ever need in order to keep himself sharp than by taking the occasional big risk? But of course there was the lure of a possible huge bonus here – the hope of seeing her again just one more time.

The outlaw was an optimist these days despite being hunted all over the territory, or even the fact that now the bunch seemed to be drifting slowly apart.

All this stemmed from the kidnapping.

That had been solely Clanton's idea and when he'd arbitrarily decided to return Lisa Randolph to her father without consulting them, that was when major cracks had begun to appear in the bunch.

Such a situation might have been important to him once. Not now. For the Lisa Randolph experience had resulted in big changes both to his thinking and his life.

Which was how come he was riding solo today.

He had cut the bunch adrift tonight in order to attempt to see her alone again to discover if she might possibly feel a little like the way he'd come to feel about her. . . .

Should this miracle happen he believed he could take on the world, make any changes and maybe even go straight and one day get to hang up the .45s. Who could tell?

Meantime every instinct warned that the old territory was changing, maybe forever. The government and the lawmakers were growing stronger by the day and wouldn't quit until they had rounded up the last of the wild boys and had a sheriff posted in every hick town boasting fifty citizens or more.

He'd first foreseen this coming when Vallery and his dog pack of Capital City blue jackets had hounded them relentlessly out in his once-secure Panhandles.

Sure, times were a-changing, and he realized he'd accelerated that change the day he kidnapped the governor's daughter. The kidnapping, which had been intended to bring Randolph to his knees, had had the reverse effect. It had backfired on him and and it was a bitter pill to swallow to see how many once-loyal supporters had switched and begun cheering for Vallery of late.

He'd believed he could claw his way back to popularity until finally realizing he'd simply made too many enemies. Now the South and a new life were calling.

But there would be one final display of the old Sonny Boy's dash and tearaway style before he stepped from centre stage. But if luck was with him tonight and his nerve held true . . . then, if nothing else, there might be one last romantic meeting – just for the memories.

It was dusk when the lone horseman clattered across the stone bridge on the capital's south-western side. Softly upon the evening air came the sweet chimes of the angelus and when the horse's hoofs rattled upon the ancient cobblestones of the Square of Heroes his cautious side whispered, 'Last chance to turn back.' Yet he only smiled and kept right on, softly humming an old Mexican tune whose lead line was, 'Never ride back. . . .'

He pushed on.

All streets here led to the great *placita* where the governor's mansion stood massively on one side with markets, dance halls and mescal dives on the other. He told himself he was feeling lucky and saw no reason why his good fortune shouldn't hold here as it had always done back in the Panhandles, even when it seemed half the territory was chasing him.

It all had to do with confidence and he'd always been loaded with it.

He glanced down at his outfit; peasant smock, baggy pants, big heavy sandals. No sign of the lethal Colt strapped around his slender middle. His hat was a rattan sombrero and his bronzed skin had been darkened with coffee grounds to make him better resemble a native than a gringo desperado.

He tingled with excitement as his way led through the poor quarter, aware that not only did he look like a native but felt like one, simple and harmless, just another young man out for a good time.

The dry trampled grass gave out and he felt the road start to mix with gravel and dirt. Huddled adobe houses moved slowly past. This part of the city was old – nobody knew just how old. It had stood too long to be changed by new people or new governors. When a little ragged kid shot past him on flying bare feet he saw himself before the world turned cruel and he'd picked up a gun, never to put it down again.

Reining in before the brightly lit pavilion where music was spilling out, he inhaled deeply. Stepping down and flipping an urchin a coin to take care of his horse, he was acutely aware of his danger but far more of the excitement. He muttered, 'She will be here . . . she has to be. . . .'

And she was.

He sighted her as soon as he'd ducked under the entrance canopy and paid an ugly man his twenty cents admission. She was amongst a group on the far side of the plank-board dance floor where a self-important official was sprinkling sawdust for the dancers, and was reassuring himself how simple it all really was when someone said, 'Take off your hat.'

The man standing before him was white, and he sniffed as he looked him up and down.

'My hat?' Clanton said, and felt that tingle he got whenever challenged by authority. 'Maybe you'd like to take it off me—?' he began, then stopped himself in time as the man's face darkened. 'Oh, sure, the hat,' he smiled and did as ordered, staring the man straight in the eye as if daring him to link this inno-cent-looking young stranger in his fancy Mexican costume with the most wanted outlaw in the land. 'Thank you, sir.'

'They should be kept out,' he heard the official mutter as he moved on, and Sonny Boy's darkened features wreathed in a smile. The man was arrogant and officious, yet he could picture him suffering a seizure were he to realize who it was he'd just unwittingly admitted to the big night which officialdom had put on to celebrate the safe return of their very own 'princess'.

Anonymous amongst the ebullient crowd surrounding the floor-boarded dance area, he stood on his toes to see over the heads before him and the last traces of uncertainty and doubt faded and were gone.

And knew now she must respond the way he hoped; he wasn't doubting it any longer.

For hadn't he cared for and protected her from the others before finally demonstrating how he felt in spiriting her out of the camp and handing her life and freedom back to her on a silver platter by returning her to the capital?

But at that time he'd believed that was the last time he would ever see her.

And maybe it would have been but for that night in the Panhandles several days later when he'd sat working his way steadily through a fifth of rye whiskey in a mountain-back hell-hole, and realized what had actually happened to him without his even being aware of it.

He had fallen in love.

And yet he had carelessly returned her to the fortress of Capital City. What a fool he must have been! He'd brooded several days until sighting the poster advertising the Governor's Ball – and knew in an instant then what he would and must do.

Come see her again.

It could be done. For who would imagine he'd dare come within twenty miles of a place where troopers, lawmen and militiamen were thick upon the ground?

He could disguise himself and come visiting. Simple!

He was vaguely aware he'd been jostled by somebody and again heard someone mutter, 'They should be kept out,' loud enough for him to hear. He paid no attention as he scanned the faces of the dancers. And suddenly there she was yonder by a richly ornamented trestle-table, obviously the centrepiece of a group of young women vying for the attention of young officers of the militia and army, along with what plainly was the cream of Capital City society.

His heart began to thud and when he heard her laugh his wrists tingled with excitement.

He stopped, and when the orchestra struck up a waltz tune she reappeared in the arms of a tall man with thick black hair who had his back to him.

Clanton shook his head and forced a grin. So, what had he expected? Of course she'd be dancing – she would be the most sought-after partner here tonight. But he would cut in – others were doing so. He started forward as the couple turned gracefully and the lights fell on her partner's face.

He froze as he watched Dev Vallery touch the back of his hand to Lisa Randolph's cheek and saw her smile up into his face then lean her head against his chest.

And instantly realized he was watching two people in love!

How long he remained frozen there with one hand around his gun handle he would never know.

He didn't even recall making his stumbling way back through the crowd to lurch out into the night. All he knew was that within the space of just one day he'd climbed impossible heights of hope only to come crashing down lower than Sonny Boy Clanton had ever been.

What a fool he'd been!

That was the mantra that drummed in his head as he somehow found where he'd left his horse and swung up to point its ugly nose back towards the Square of Heroes.

And thought now: how could a man be such a fool?

'Hey you, where the hell do you think you're going?'

The voice that jolted him back to reality saw him blink down at two plaza sentries blocking his way. Beyond them were two uniformed outriders, and in the background a heavy black carriage drawn by four stylish horses.

'Huh?' he grunted vaguely, still moving forwards.

The closer man moved swiftly to seize his mount by the throat strap and drag it to a halt. His companion cursed;

'Damned drunk!' he yelled. 'Make way for the governor, you fool!'

Clanton was coming out of the shock and sickness now. He grew conscious of the angry faces, recognized the impressive vehicle slowly turning before him to swing in the direction of the marquee as the governor's carriage in all its glittering splendour.

Like a man in a trance, as a detached onlooker he saw his big Colt gushing gun flame and felt it bucking against the crotch of his hand as the great head-jolting blasts shook the plaza. He was shooting over their heads and saw the first man let go of the horse and dive to ground with hands clapped over his head, howling in terror.

He raked viciously with spur to charge the second man down before he could clear his revolver. The body went under the hoofs and the horse stumbled but regained its balance to break into full gallop. Barely avoiding rearing carriage horses, Clanton swivelled in his saddle and heard his name shouted again and again as he punched shot after shot into the sky to send men diving wildly for the cover of the violently rocking carriage. Until his six-gun ran empty and he was galloping furiously for the great curved archway leading out of the square and onto the vast darkened plain beyond.

He made it into the open unscathed, ducking and weaving in the saddle now as gunfire from the walls above reached out for him. Soon the bullets were falling short and the horse responded when he dug with his spurs to be swiftly engulfed by the growling electrical storm rolling in off the plains.

CHAPTER 8

POSSE

'How is he, Lisa?' Vallery asked quickly as the girl emerged from Randolph's chambers, closing the door behind her.

'I'm sure he'll be fine, Dev. The doctor says Father was simply badly shaken up when the coach crashed.' She forced a smile. 'He's stronger than he looks, I always think.'

'Needs to be these days.'

Lisa crossed to the windows overlooking the town square. It was the following day and the scene below appeared much the same as any other day. On the surface. Yet in reality it was totally different. In the space of just a handful of violent minutes last night, the feeling almost of complacency that had descended in the wake of recent turmoil had been

111

brutally shattered with one man wounded and three Capital City guards laid up in hospital with minor injuries sustained in the gun battle upon the square.

Sonny Boy Clanton had come calling.

A maid brought coffee and the couple sat in a deep windowseat to drink. Vallery gazed directly across at the sector where the gunplay had erupted, his expression pensive. Lisa continued to study him in silence.

At length he grew aware of her attention and arched a questioning eyebrow. 'What is it?'

'I was just thinking . . . you are very quiet this morning.'

He shrugged. 'Hardly surprising, is it? I mean, just when we were thinking that maybe the hellions had had a bellyful of being chased and hounded all over the county, Sonny Boy shows up right here and cuts loose. I sure find that plenty worrisome.'

'So do I. Who wouldn't? But . . . but I just hoped there might be a positive side to it, Dev.'

'Such as?'

She dropped her gaze. She looked lovely as usual, he mused, even if pale and worried-looking. He wasn't surprised.

'Well . . . I suppose I was just hoping that because of what happened you might decide to stay on a little longer?'

Vallery rose and commenced pacing the room.

'Lisa, I came here to Capital City because—'

'I know, Dev,' she interrupted, rising quickly. 'To help us out in a crisis – which you did, brilliantly. Possibly Sonny may have simply meant to return me to safety all along, yet I realized while I was being held that your presence here certainly influenced his decision to set me free.' She paused, then added quietly, 'That and the other thing. . . .'

He looked up. 'The other thing, Lisa?'

She looked away. Her voice was soft. 'I think he must have fallen in love with me.'

The notion jolted him. At first. Yet almost immediately he felt himself beginning to understand. And remembered how astonished he'd been when Lisa had been set free. For Sonny Boy didn't play that way; if he set out on a course, he stuck to it. He knew fear would never have prompted Lisa's release, but love might explain it.

They stood looking at one another, each deep in thought. Then Lisa began to speak but a broke off as knuckles sounded on the hallway door.

'Come!' she called, and Colonel Nathan Dater came striding into the room, sweeping feathered hat from his head and bowing with an old world flourish.

'Miss Randolph, er, Vallery. I trust I find you both well, and the governor of course . . . or as well as might be expected in his case, that is?'

There was a momentary silence. For like the man

113

or not, Dater had a powerful presence. Rumours continued to circulate that the militia commander was continuing to wage an underhand campaign amongst spheres of political influence to promote himself as replacement governor. 'The only man strong enough to impose genuine law and order in the territory!' was his unofficial slogan.

For this and other reasons Lisa mistrusted the man deeply. Yet, as ever, she was courteous and informed Dater that her father was in good health and merely badly shaken.

There was no gauging how this information affected Dater, if at all. There was about him today, as always, an air of suppressed force and aggression.

'Was there something else, Colonel?' Lisa asked after a lengthy silence, her voice tinged with impatience.

There certainly was. Dater had come seeking her personal account of last night's events – if she would be so kind?

Vallery reacted sharply.

'She's told you all you need to know,' he said testily. 'Maybe you'd be better employed heading out into the Panhandles searching for Sonny Boy?'

Dater's hard eyes glittered. He inhaled deeply. The two men had never hit it off. Dater was never prepared to overlook Vallery's background or accept his reformation. In turn, Dev regarded the militia

commander as a potentially dangerous man of reckless ambition.

'You know something, mister?' Dater said tightly. 'I
might be the only one who's noticed that ever since
you showed back here things have been a damn sight
worse than they were before, which tells me that—'

He broke off as the door to the bedchamber
opened and the governor appeared. He was fully
dressed but noticeably paler than usual.

Greetings between governor and militia commander were stiff and formal, as always. Randolph had
learned from different sources recently that Colonel
Dater's aspirations to become governor were seen to
be growing more overt in many circles. It was on
public record with the Territorial Attorney's Office
that he'd officially applied for permission to hunt
down the Clanton bunch 'without interference from
Capital City' – meaning the governor. Should this be
granted it would seriously undermine Randolph's
authority.

Vallery lighted a cigar and paced to and fro as the
two men tersely reviewed the night's events. He
didn't show much interest, not because he was
unconcerned about the violence involving Sonny
Boy but simply because his thoughts were elsewhere.
And were weighty.

Yesterday he'd been preoccupied by the feeling
he'd been away from the spread too long and should

be on his way home, despite the responsibilty he felt towards Lisa.

All that had changed overnight.

For disturbing as Sonny Boy's reappearance had been, something of even greater significance for Vallery had taken place just prior to the gunplay.

It happened when he and Lisa were innocently gliding around to the music of the five-piece orchestra that they'd suddenly found themselves gazing into one another's eyes and realizing that virtually everything had changed between them – the leap from friendship to something much stronger. It had struck so overwhelmingly that even in the aftermath of the Sonny Boy chaos they'd sat talking until the small hours and Dev had awoken that morning aware that his life would never be the same again.

He realized that he'd fallen in love and that, for her safety, he must remain here and see Sonny Boy brought to justice.

The spread could look after itself.

Dev Vallery's duty lay right here and no place else.

Deep in thought, he didn't even hear Dater call to him from across the room, the first time. When he didn't respond the man spoke again, sharply this time. Too sharp to Dev's ear.

'You're not on the parade ground bullying a bunch of recruits now, Dater, so guard your tongue!' he fired back.

The officer flushed darkly and made to retort but Dev deliberately spoke over him. 'Just what is it you want, Colonel?'

Dater was angry but a warning gesture from Randolph caused the man to rein in his temper. 'I've requested the governor make official my request that you join my company as chief scout immediately during my renewed campaign to destroy Clanton and his gang, once and for all. My scouts have done some fine work in recent days and are certain they have picked up on the gang's scent in the south by south-eastern sector of the Wilderness. I'm convinced if we follow this up immediately it could well result in success. I trust you have no objections?'

'What do you say, Dev? I know it's one hell of a lot but—'

'It's all right, Governor.' Vallery had reached his decision instantly. Nothing of worth could be achieved or attempted until Sonny Boy was behind bars. He thrust out his hand. 'I'll bring Sonny Boy in for you. Matter of fact I might have a hunch where the bunch could be headed right now, in light of what Dater just reported. That south-eastern sector of the badlands is some place he and I used to wander back in the old days after we got sick of raising hell and posses pushing us too close. . . .'

The governor's fierce grip said it all and an animated Dater clapped Dev's shoulder with a broad smile of genuine relief. But Lisa simply looked shocked.

'But, Dev, you told me just last night that you don't believe anybody can catch Sonny. How has that changed?'

'That was last night, Lisa. But in light of what Dater just reported, I might even have a hunch where he's making for now.' He swung back to the governor. 'I know this man better than anyone and if Sonny's reign can be ended, it must be now.' He paused. 'Sorry, Lisa.'

Lisa would understand in time, he told himself as he left a short time later to make ready. He could only hope he might live to see that day. For no matter how this played out, Sonny would surely prove to be the most dangerous man he'd ever hunted.

It was the toughest three days the manhunters had ever lived through.

Vallery drove them like galley slaves. The hand-picked party of fifteen which he'd first selected then personally led from Capital City were all volunteers. But none had realized what lay ahead during those brutal days of sign-reading and hard riding that took them from Clantonville Creek in the south to the arid plains which lay within sight of the mighty Mile High Escarpment to the north.

During the ride they saw nothing of their quarry

and Vallery didn't expect there to be. For from the moment he'd realized Sonny Boy's bunch had swung away from the east to follow an ancient Indian track angling north, he'd seized upon a hunch and had run with it.

He was guessing where the gang was headed now and cut across country. His objective could be an old Comanche trail which wound its way up from the low plains to the frowning brow of the landmark escarpment which brooded two thousand feet above the level of the plains.

If he guessed right, and Sonny was making for that perilous track, their superior numbers backed up with the advantage of surprise might well see them get to mount an ambush that would mark the end of the wild bunch.

He frowned.

Of course, if wrong, then his enemies and all those Sonny Boy supporters back at Capital City might be proven right. When they were quitting the capital the gamblers had already been making wagers that the posse would not catch Sonny Boy either this week or in the next ten years.

It was all familiar to Sonny Boy Clanton: the single-horse winding trail, the brooding buttes and the heat rippling across an immensity of brassy blue sky. He knew he should feel relieved and triumphant as his horse reared spiritedly beneath him and jingled its head harness, but all he felt was grim.

Last time he'd been forced to seek sanctuary up to the great rim he'd been half-hellion and half-hero to an entire county. Today it felt much more like most everybody was against him following the shootup at Capital City.

He'd always felt the Capital man in the street looked upon him as more a charming rascal than a bloody handed outlaw . . . like Lord, for instance. But not any longer.

He'd slipped from his pedestal and mourned to think how he'd fallen so low. Abducting the governor's daughter had proven a huge mistake and signalled the first major plunge in his popularity, but he had managed to reclaim some ground by returning Lisa unharmed.

But after that had come the slippery-slide – Dad Matthews, Sim Ollinger, a panhandler he'd gunned down like a dog over at Los Nobles. Crimes, outbursts of rage, even maybe a hint of madness now and then.

Yet still not enough negatives to turn all Deaf Smith County against him. That hadn't happened until the night he disguised himself in order to get to see Lisa again in the hope he might through her, maybe get to give himself a genuine reason to want to go on living. Maybe turn over a new leaf, apply for a pardon, dump the bunch and go straight the way Dev had done.

And what a mockery and disaster that had turned out to be. . . .

He shook his head and massaged his jaw, the horse rolling the dark jewel of its eye backwards to look at him.

He spat and sleeved his mouth as he saw again the love glowing in her beautiful eyes – not for Sonny Boy but for another man. Dev Vallery!

He took out a stogie and fired it into life with a sweep of a lucifer. The brief flare of the match illuminated a face still young yet suddenly as old as the stones of time.

But at least he understood how things were – and how they would be.

That look he'd seen her give Dev meant Sonny would have to kill his ex-pard sooner or later if he was to retain any pride. But there'd been no time to go after Vallery after the governor dispatched Dater and the militia and the manhunters to pursue him so remorselessly. They had been camped on his tracks almost a week now, driving him loco. But of course it was Vallery who posed the the threat. For Dev knew him too well, knew his tricks and many of his secret hideaways and trails. Even the way he thought at times.

Hell! The man knew him so damn well that by this

Sonny Boy the fearless had no option but run and keep running, for now. He'd led the possemen a good roundabout chase but they were sticking on his trail as never before.

It was now a situation requiring desperate measures – and he knew exactly where he was heading.

He knew of a precipitous and dangerous horse-trail rising from hostile redskin country in the south-east that climbed two thousand feet high where they'd be far out of the reach of any lick-spittle posse – Dater the son of a bitch, and Judas Vallery . . . along with those running-dog towners and lawmen they had riding with them.

He licked his lips and gusted cigar smoke into the still night air.

Everywhere he looked these days – enemies. The world hated him, but the world was yet to discover what real hate could be like.

Eventually he might quit the county but not before some outstanding accounts were settled.

'Forward ho!' he bawled suddenly at the top of his lungs and the riders moved on.

Travelling at head of the band now swollen to a dozen, Sonny Boy guided his horse down to dried-out Clayton Creek then climbed the far bank. Directly behind him rode Marlon Lord flanked by Pomeroy, Rutherford and Lincoln, all well mounted and bristling with arms.

His henchmen, although happy to be away from Fort Supply, rode mostly in silence. But some of the new recruits bringing up the rear were in high spirits and still elated to have been selected by Sonny Boy to ride with them after he realized he might need reinforcements in light of the size and tenacity of that stinking posse – wherever the hell it might be right now!

The young ones were all guntippers or hellraisers of one stripe or another. Clanton was yet to tell them his plan to launch a massive campaign of rustling and robbery the like of which Deaf Smith County had never seen, just so soon as they'd shaken this posse. Yet they wouldn't have been alarmed even if they had known, for they were young and immortal just like Sonny Boy. Weren't they?

After an hour the trail steadily grew rougher and narrower, forcing the cavalcade to maintain single file. They finally surmounted a switch back ridge then dusted down into a pretty little valley. Half the valley was encircled by red sandstone. At one spot, huge oaks grew from the base of the cliff face with massive branches leaning far out over pools of sweet water.

It was a tranquil and sylvan scene so much in contrast with their situation.

Clanton led them to the creek where they watered

their mounts and fashioned brown-paper cigarettes before moving on.

The trail eventually began to climb steeply and the riders wound their way between echoing stone cliffs before the way opened up suddenly, and high above they glimpsed a mighty plateau where mesquite studded the sunwashed crests. But directly ahead stood the jaws of a narrow pass which compressed their trail to single-horse width.

'This Sawtooth?' inquired the broken-beaked outlaw riding behind Clanton.

'Damn right it is. When we get through there we'll be better than halfway up to the Mile High Escarpment and the Divide. No stinking posse will ever track us up there . . . we can rest up along the Divide . . . where it's cool even this time of the year . . . cool and peaceful.'

'Cool and peaceful sounds fine, Sonny Boy.'

Had Sonny Boy glanced up through the grey limbs of the giant, cliff-side oak as he passed beneath he might have glimpsed a hard bronzed face staring down at him through a luxurious cluster of leaves.

But he didn't look up. None of them did.

CHAPTER 9

SEIZE THE DAY!

Smoke trickled from Dev Vallery's lips and wisped away on the gusting wind.

He raised his cigarillo and drew deeply again, savouring the good taste of the tobacco which dulled that sensation of the calm before the storm.

A trooper scurried past below his lookout position to cross the open shelf of blue rock, clutching his rifle tightly with both hands. The man propped sharply when Dater suddenly came erect to signal to him with a curt gesture. Wordlessly he directed him to a defensive position where already a line of grim riflemen lay sprawled belly-flat behind a scatter of ancient granite boulders, their cocked and ready rifles all trained upon the mouth of the pass below.

Waiting to kill.

Vallery felt almost relaxed now that the brutal days of pursuit were finally behind – ahead now only the unknown.

Would the Sonny Boys fight or quit when they realized they didn't stand a hope in hell?

He'd first become aware that their gruelling pursuit of their quarry across a hundred miles of wild and unmapped badlands country was about to bear fruit when his field glasses had finally picked up the outlaw cavalcade far across the plains curving directly northwards for Sawtooth Pass.

That name and place meant nothing to his possemen, nor even the veterans. It would not have meant anything to Dev either but for an incident several years earlier when he and Clanton were on the run from an angry posse. Fortune saw them cross trails with an old sourdough pard from the Broken Twist country who'd spirited them away to the secret precipitous trail which climbed to the top of the mighty escarpment through the previously unknown and unsuspected Sawtooth Pass.

Vallery had never had reason to return until yesterday after finally picking up the dust of Sonny and his bunch and had immediately realized they meant to ascend the Escarpment via Sawtooth – the only exit route from the badlands flats up to that lofty rim within thirty miles.

He'd led his party at the gallop to reach Sawtooth well ahead of the gang, and promptly led them up through that narrow pass to reach Bluestone Plateau, a natural ambush site.

Of course there had always been the risk Sonny might change his mind and veer away from Sawtooth, but it hadn't happened. And now he felt a nerve in his neck began to pulse as the first faint sounds of hoofs striking rock told him riders were finally entering Sawtooth Pass . . . climbing for the plateau.

He and Sonny face to face – at last.

He'd never wanted it to come to this.

But the possemen's strength in this deadly game would be the advantages of position and surprise. Add a modicum of luck backed up by good shooting and the showdown could be all over within mere minutes. Maybe. . . .

Whichever way it went, the one thing certain was that it would be bloody.

Vallery stiffened. The bobbing head of a climbing horse had just appeared above the mouth of the pass and within moments man and rider were fully visible, steel-shod hoofs ringing sharply against the flinty bluestone surface of the plateau.

Some distance off to his right a camouflaged Dater raised his right arm and paused, ready to give the signal that would let slip the dogs of death.

His arm fell and it began.

The hatchet-faced outlaw dropped before the driving impact of a .32 soft-nosed slug fired at almost point blank range and his body tumbled over a wounded fighter desperately crawling for cover directly below Vallery's position.

In mere moments the one-sided battle between possemen and outlaws still dazed and disoriented by the ferocity of the ambush, climbed to a fierce and clashing crescendo of arms which held, seemingly forever, then abruptly dropped away in intensity with the battleground littered with dead and wounded men and Sonny Boy's bloodied survivors desperately scrabbling for cover that wasn't really to be found.

It should have been a moment of ultimate triumph for Colonel Nathan Dater, yet even as he watched murderous volleys ripping through outlaw horsemen bringing the onset of panic amongst the enemy, his thoughts were distracting him from the here and now.

He was permitting himself to imagine the triumphal return to Capital City with the excitement and the accolades – and thunderous acclaim for the governor's greatest victory.

Yet he knew that that day must surely prove to be Randolph's, not his own. For wasn't Randolph everyman's hero while Nathan Dater was just the hated militia boss who could win battles but never accolades?

But wasn't there a way that all the acclaim and prestige would devolve upon himself with nothing left over for Randolph to benefit by – thus opening up his pathway to the governorship?

Then suddenly more wild-eyed outlaws both mounted and afoot were erupting from the pass to fan out across the plateau behind bucking guns . . . and he cleared his mind of everything else but the here and now.

His hand jerked trigger and the shot was rewarded by a gurgling death cry from a shattered throat – and the slaughter climaxed again.

It was brief and brutal even for such a time and place.

But the possemen held positional advantage from the outset and swiftly attained full supremacy with a maelstrom of howling lead until dead and wounded littered the bloodied earth and riderless mounts screamed in terror and pain with a sound straight out of hell.

Across the clearing Dev Vallery sat his saddle without even a gun in hand, an onlooker in a game called Death.

And yet he felt curiously detached from it all as the carnage roared to a climax and the upper reaches of Sawtooth Pass trembled and shook to the madness of total conflict.

Youthful desperadoes tumbled from their saddles under those shattering volleys, some without even getting a shot away, others triggering insanely as they fell. Yet several of the swiftest and most nimble leapt to ground to make scant cover from where they instantly began blasting back at the ambushers.

A bearded killer with eyes blazing like buggy lamps came spurring across the plateau with a long-barrelled .45-.40 reaching out before him to home in on an ambusher who bobbed up in order to get a better sighting. The horseman triggered twice and the ambusher fell. But a trooper cut loose and three soft-nosed slugs wrote a bloody pattern across the horseman's gaping mouth. Hitting dirt, he floundered like a drowning fish, dying with spurs ripping earth that turned crimson beneath him.

Chaos ruled on every side now with dust and smoke rising in a vast angry pall until both sides grew fogged and indistinct in the frenzied action of warring parties.

And all the while Vallery watched and wished bitterly it might have been different.

But the prize here was the future peace of the territory – and in that he fiercely believed.

And those warring guns did roar.

By this, horses and men were choking on smoke and blood and figures threshed in the dust. A pair of disoriented outlaws ran blindly through a wall of gunsmoke only to blunder into a volley of posse-men's lead that scythed their legs from under them.

A Fort Supply recruit dashed after a loose horse, leapt astride like a redskin and made thirty racing yards before the crossfire caught up with him and punched him from the saddle with the horse going down on its nose moments later.

At the heart of the deadliest mêlée were men of the calibre of Marlon Lord and Fritz Lincoln, the gunslingers costing their adversaries dear until finally overrun by sheer numbers and taken captive.

It couldn't last after that, and didn't.

Too many outlaws had fallen and in the final phase the ambushers mounted a charge with such ferocity that the desperate cry rose from the enemy ranks; 'We surrender!'

Instantly Vallery drew his Colt and pumped three evenly spaced shots into the sky. 'Hold your fire!' he roared at the top of his lungs and one by one the guns eased off to fall quickly silent.

The quiet was eerie, deep and ghost-like. But not for long. Responding to an order from Dater the outlaw survivors began to stagger out from cover, tossing aside overheated weapons and blinking from the violent shock of it all while the low sounds of moaning rose on all sides.

Somehow Vallery was not surprised when he

glimpsed the figure of a disarmed Marlon Lord with a trooper's weapon in his back emerge from the gun fog, trailed by a battle-weary Fritz Lincoln.

Though victory was his, Dater waited until dust and gunsmoke had cleared away before finally emerging from cover to begin barking orders, then striding across to where Vallery was standing.

'You see any sign of Clanton, Vallery?'

Dev shook his head and Dater hurried off to inspect a line of still figures sprawled in the bloodied grass.

But within a minute the word spread, seemingly to reach everybody at the same moment.

Sonny Boy Clanton was nowhere to be found!

Dragging hungrily on a smoke, Vallery realized he wasn't surprised. How many times in the past had he known Sonny to escape when it seemed impossible? He'd not wanted him to die here yet had hoped to see him taken in order that a final peace might be guaranteed.

He didn't bother joining the frantic search. Instinct told him Sonny was gone. And he doubted they would ever see him again, not if he understood the abilities of the man he'd once called friend. . . .

'I want to see that bastard's corpse!' Dater was roaring in the background. Then he approached the cavvy of prisoners with a revolver in his fist, and he jammed the muzzle against a tall prisoner's heart.

'But . . . at least we've got you for the gallows by God and by Judas . . . scum!'

Marlon Lord turned his head and spat contemptuously. 'If you're fixing to shoot then shoot and be damned!' he growled.

'The shooting's over. Put that thing away!'

Dater twisted as Vallery approached. His face coloured hectically. 'Just who in hell do you think you're ordering around, Vallery?'

Dev ignored him to fix Lord with a cold stare. 'Where's Sonny?'

At that moment Sergeant Coe came lumbering forward, red-faced and sweaty. He threw a clumsy salute.

'That man just ain't here nohow, Colonel. He's clear got away on us!'

'I don't believe it!' Dater croaked. 'I won't!' His disbelieving gaze focused upon Lord. 'How? You must know.'

Lord shrugged, indifferent to it all now. 'He went out under his horse's belly, of course, Injun style, hanging onto the belly band. Only non-Comanche I ever knew could do that.' Then the gunman's expression changed dramatically. 'Dirty low-down bastard ran out on us and left us hanging. I never figured to see the day.'

'Sonny should never have quit on us that way,' a wounded outlaw insisted. 'He—'

'Shut your scum mouth!' Dater spat, fighting rage and bitter disappointment. 'Make up a detail and go search some more!'

Men promptly responded but within minutes even Dater knew it was useless. It was then that victors and vanquished alike seemed to join with all those Deaf Smith County folk who had long believed the Devil himself protected Sonny Boy Clanton.

The lone rider whistled a tune through his teeth as he wrapped a ripped-off shirtsleeve around the bullet crease in his left thigh. His side ached, too, where a posseman's slug had hit home.

He sat in the shade of a leafy cottonwood five miles north-west of Sawtooth Pass deep in his famil- iar Panhandles. He grunted in satisfaction as he tied a knot in the bandaging then got to his feet to test it. It was a mite sore but nothing much. He'd had worse. Plenty worse.

He filled leather effortlessly and pushed off along an ancient Indian track with a freshly lit cigarette dangling from his lips.

He rode without guilt or regret and would be astonished should he be expected to feel different.

And yet, sobering momentarily, he realized he'd finally finished with Deaf Smith County. The old bunch was gone and he felt free as he'd not done in years. He would start off fresh in some far place where folks would look up to him as they'd once done here.

Sure, that's what he would do.

But . . . not quite yet. There was one thing he must do before he headed for Mexico . . . a difficult and dangerous thing to be sure, yet it was something that must last him a lifetime.

He nodded.

Hatreds and old scores no longer drove him as before. For everything had changed the day Sonny Boy dreamed up the big idea to capture the governor's daughter, yet instead had surrendered his own freedom to something called love.

Yet he could and would survive, but would only ever be truly safe again after he headed south until he was as far from Capital City and a girl named Lisa as a man could travel.

He nodded. Smart thinking that, Sonny Boy. Yet smartness or common sense were now his foes, not friends. For he could never leave without one last goodbye . . . maybe even a last touch and a look from sparkling eyes that must sustain him for the rest of his lonely life.

The plan already taking shape in his mind was loco. He realized that. But as most of his life had been lived on the crazy side this held no fears.

He made it all sound simple; ride to Capital City, find a way to get to see her if even for just one immortal moment – then, California here I come!'

One last defiant roll of the dice, Sonny Boy!

'I'm not asking you to change your mind, mister. I'm ordering!'

All conversation ceased as Dater's raised voice caused heads to turn and watch as Vallery calmly fitted boot to stirrup then swung astride just as though the militia boss hadn't even spoken.

He settled into his saddle and gazed down. 'You've won a big victory here today, Colonel, and I handed it to you on a platter. So don't be a fool and foul it up now. I answer to the governor and only him, like you know. I'm on my way to report back to him and he'll only hear the truth about what happened here from me. But that will be enough to boost you to top dog at Capital City when you get there with your prisoners, so what are you griping about?'

His gesture encompassed the campsite.

'You've got plenty men to boss about here, you don't need one more.'

'But—'

That was all Vallery heard as he kicked his horse into a lope and rode from the camp with the morning sun at his back. Red-faced and angry, the colonel fiddled with the handle of his big Services revolver at his hip but did not draw. He watched Vallery ride on until he dropped from sight without looking back.

Both militiamen and prisoners camped by a crooked creek thirty miles south-east of the capital that night while the colonel took supper alone by his own private fire.

Dater was considering his entire future.

This was nothing new for he'd always been a man of far-reaching ambition. But tonight he was seeing himself and his future in the harsh light of reality, maybe for the first time ever.

His reality was ugly and confronting.

Following years marked by both failures and successes he had finally destroyed the Clanton bunch and the fact that Clanton himself had escaped was now seemingly unimportant in the wake of Sawtooth Pass.

The victory should make the colonel the hero of the hour. But it had not and would not. Ever. He would never rise to where he wanted to be on popular acclaim – therefore he must seize the prize.

Tonight the colonel wanted it all, including the ultimate reward.

Randolph's job.

For the governor would surely claim this triumph as his own while Dater's unpopularity would ensure he would forever remain where he was right now – respected but hated, and the eternal Number Two.

He took his emotions for a walk and caught sight of Marlon Lord pacing to and fro, dragging his leg irons like a dangerous beast, which in many ways he was. Lincoln was just a dim shadow, skulking in the gloom of the prisoners' enclosure.

Dater halted and Lord's eyes glittered with hatred.

'Can't sleep, Dater? That's the penalty you pay for the dirty work you did for Randolph.'

Dater moved closer – yet not too close.

'You hate everybody, don't you, killer? The law, Vallery . . . even Governor Randolph. What's the governor ever done to you that anybody else wouldn't, given half a chance?'

'You've got to be jesting, Dater. What's he done – you ask? That son of a whore has done little else but try to kill me ever since he took over. I've lost close pards every year to him but never so many at one time like I did today. He said when he took over he'd rid the territory of guys like me, but didn't even look like getting anywhere close to that, until yesterday. All those good buddies . . . gone. And you're asking me why I want him dead—'

'Talk is cheap, gunslinger—' Dater began, then fell silent with a jolt, staring. The gunman's hatred was palpable, so much so that Dater suddenly felt a leaping sensation within him as a crazy thought took hold.

Get rid of the governor right now while the whole capital was in a turmoil of excitement.

Was this a once-in-a-lifetime opportunity or a

ticket to the gallows?

Whatever, he knew he could not stop now. 'And I suppose if you were free tonight nothing would stop you slipping into Capital City and doing what you know you should have done long ago, but didn't? Namely, pay Randolph out for all he's cost you?'

He waited breathlessly, shocked by his own recklessness. Yet the prisoner appeared laconic, ice cool. 'I could kill that bastard easy, given half a chance . . . if that is what you're asking. And if you're serious, Dater, I can tell you it'd be like taking candy from a kid.'

Dater stood transfixed. Countless times he'd plotted the death of Randolph in his thoughts yet in the end it had always appeared impossible . . . until that crazy moment as Lord's glitter-eyed intensity seemed to convince him that it was all possible – if he only had the courage to reach that high. . . .

If.

He knew it was the moment of a lifetime as he reached out and grasped Marlon Lord's right hand and felt an electrifying jolt pass between them.

Colonel Dater realized he was ready to seize the day!

CHAPTER 10

DEATH THE DEALER

The capital's south side was a fetid sprawl of ramshackle dwellings, narrow, twisting streets and a criss-crossing maze of gloomy alleyways polluted by the eternal stench of a restless and careless humanity. Down here it was hogs in the street, holes in the roof, cheap booze in wild excess and a cynical belief in the philosophy that if today had been bad then tomorrow would surely be ten times worse. Shove your hand in and pull back a stub!

Sonny Boy Clanton smiled beneath his tugged-down hatbrim as he made his way along the shadowy walk. He knew what he was doing was loco yet the whole thing appealed to him – helped take his mind off the wounds he'd taken at the Sawtooth. His recklessness always gave him an edge and could make him feel immortal at times.

Even the squalid downtown appeared excited and overcrowded tonight – they were still celebrating the news of the victory over the Sonny Boys gang out east.

While the outlaw whose fall they were cheering was swaggering past them unnoticed down here beneath a flapping bum's coat. This had worked well before when he'd infiltrated Capital City on some bloody business or other, and he knew it would not fail him tonight.

His last night in Capital City . . . and the night they would remember as Sonny Boy's.

He halted abruptly, hand going to his temple. He was hot as hell, he realized. Bullet wounds could cause a fever and he had both . . . wound and fever. It had been the posseman's slug in his side that convinced him he wanted to escape alive from Sawtooth Pass. That, and the startling realization he'd not really wanted to kill any of the ambushers – not even Dev.

And understood at last just how much he'd changed – and all due to her. She was the one who'd taken the devil out of Sonny Boy Clanton, and it had taken him all this time to figure that. With luck, he'd

141

killed his last man . . . but you never could tell. . . .

He took a powerful swig from a hip flask and felt strong again.

A dim figure emerged from a shrouded alleyway some distance ahead and preceded him as he headed for the Square of Heroes. The killer offered him no more than a cursory glance and both kept walking.

Moments later he grunted and stopped on a dime. For by the light sifting down from a grimed window he'd been given a momentary glimpse of the man's face.

It was Brick Pomeroy!

Clanton's brain spun. Surely this was impossible! For he'd witnessed both Pomeroy and Lord being taken prisoner at Sawtooth! So how could the man be strolling around free as a goddamn jaybird up here at Capital City?

He went light-footed after the gloomy figure of his one-time trail pard, then continued to lag several paces behind until an alleyway beckoned on his left.

Instantly he sprang forward.

A slender arm whipped around Pomeroy's throat to cut off his startled cry as he found himself being bundled into the darkness.

Releasing his grip, Clanton spun the man around, grinning like a wolf.

'What you doing, Brick? Slummin'?'

142

Pomeroy gaped in slack jawed disbelief. 'Sonny?' Then when Clanton chuckled again, he cursed bitterly. 'Damn your dirty hide, Sonny – you ran out on us!'

'Ancient history, Brick boy. Hell, I'm pleased as all get-out to see you looking so fit and chirpy – but what's the score, pard? First, what are you doing here?'

The man turned his head and spat. 'You can go straight to hell, Sonny. I thought you were a pard but you Judased on us back there at Sawtooth—'

'Judased?' Clanton hissed. 'Don't you lay that one on me, boy.' He jabbed a finger into the man's chest, hard. 'I'm asking you again – how come you're here and walking free?'

But tough Pomeroy swatted the hand aside.

'You're all through bossing me about, Sonny. You rat on a man one day then jump up on him the next and act like nothing happened. So, whatever I'm doing has got nothing to do with you. Not now and not never!'

Pomeroy's hat spun away as Clanton's open-handed blow caught him across the face. 'You are getting uppity in your old age, Brick,' he drawled. He seized a handful of shirt front and slammed the man back against the wall. 'Start talking while you still can. I want answers!'

Pomeroy reached behind his head as though to

steady himself against the wall. When his hand flashed into sight again the cold steel of the sneak knife he'd fingered from behind his collar winked into the gloom. Clanton ducked but the eight-inch blade still found his ribcage.

Crimson spilled and Sonny Boy staggered, his face registering a brief moment's surprise. Then madness. Too swift for the eye to follow, he ripped the bloodied blade from Pomeroy's hand and drove it to the hilt in the hardcase's heart. Pomeroy stood transfixed against the wall for a moment, staring down foolishly at the haft of the knife jutting from his chest.

Then he fell.

A ragged hiss of breath escaped Clanton's lips as he stepped back and pressed a hand to his chest.

'Well, Brick, old son,' he panted, 'thought you might've finished me for a moment there . . . but scarce more than a scratch. Too bad I had to lay you out . . . like hell! But I'd sure as shooting like to know how come you got to be here. . . .'

He grimaced as he wiped his hand clean on his shirt front. He'd always hated knives even though they'd saved his life more than once. They always reminded him of that dirty mule skinner years ago . . . and that mule skinner always reminded him of Kate. . . .

'Kate. . . ?'

Knife and corpse were both forgotten as he breathed his sister's name aloud, and for a moment appeared to be some place else far away in the grimy back streets of childhood – while a corpse at his feet was still leaking crimson.

He shook his head violently. 'Better not waste any more time. Get done what you came here to do, then – *adios*!'

With an act of will he banished the pain and stepped lightly from the alleyway. He glanced both ways and strode off, not stopping until reaching the next corner.

Still plenty of folks to be seen. Celebrations booming yonder at an all-night flop house. He was about to step forward when he froze. A slim figure was passing the dim lights of Southside Saloon. The man wore a long dark weather coat and moved like a big cat.

Judas Priest! Marlon Lord! This lousy city was crawling with people who should be dead!

He watched as Lord suddenly stopped to stare about as if searching for somebody. Sonny Boy's head spun a moment until his thinking began to clarify. It was plain that if his ex-pards were wandering around here like damned tourists – someone had set them loose. But surely that could only have been Dater . . . or maybe Vallery! There could be no other explanation. But how? And even more puzzling – why? What in Hades was going on?

A twinge of pain warned that time was running out. So his ex-pards were on the loose – so he had more on his mind and big risks to take on what could prove his riskiest night ever, and maybe the craziest!

With a reckless grin and a parting glance at the distant figure of Lord, he turned in the opposite direction and hurried on. When he swung the next corner he could see the lights of the governor's palace burning bright.

Standing in the tumble down barn on the southern fringe of the capital, Colonel Dater started at the sudden sound of swift steps.

'Who it it?' he barked, hand on gun holster.

Marlon Lord's lean form appeared silently in the doorway. Dater swore.

'What are you doing back here? You're supposed to be—'

'Trouble, Dater,' Lord panted. 'Pomeroy's been killed. I just found him in an alley close by the spot where I was supposed to meet up with him.'

'Killed?' Dater couldn't believe it.

'Yeah, and that ain't the worst of it.' Lord held up a bloodstained nec kerchief, 'He was done in with his own knife, but in his hand I found this. It's Sonny's bandanna!'

Dater turned ashen. He drew back from the grue-

146

some blade as though afraid. 'Clanton? You're telling me he did it?'

'I'm saying I never saw Sonny without this neckerchief. That must mean he's here. Don't ask me how or why, but I swear to God I can feel him. He's some place in this goddamned city!'

It took all Dater's will to master his shock and begin thinking clearly again. Certainly, Pomeroy's death seemed weird and inexplicable . . . now this! What in hell was going on?

But in a moment he was back in full control. He mustn't allow anything to throw him on the most important night of his entire life.

'It doesn't change anything,' he said with a return to all his old authority. 'We'll still go through with this as planned.'

'But we've lost a man,' Lord protested. 'There's just me now.' He paused to suck in a breath and cursed. 'Look, what I'm saying is that with them palace guards and all, just two of us mightn't be enough to swing it, damnit!'

Dater's thoughts raced as he fingered the big rough coat concealing his uniform. Before quitting the high country he and his new recruits had donned greatcoats and battered head gear to prevent being identified in Capital City before the night's violent work was completed.

'We'll go ahead exactly like we planned,' he said

with all his old authority. 'I'll position myself in the palace stables and be ready to back your play if you run into any trouble. Naturally, we'll silence anyone who tries to stop us getting to Randolph. Just remember, with the governor dead there'll be no option for them but to swear me in, and once I'm occupying that position it will be my duty and my decisions that count – nobody else's. You'll have nothing to fear . . . and nor shall I.'

He broke off momentarily and felt the exhilarating power of renewed commitment.

'After we kill Randolph I'll stash my disguise and start bawling for the guards . . . while you disappear—' He had to pause to catch breath again. 'My story will be that you escaped custody, I pursued you here but arrived too late to protect the governor from you. You'll be long gone by then and we'll meet up in a week as arranged. Any questions?'

'It's still fixing to be risky,' Lord said. 'Them palace guards—'

'Will do whatever I say!' Dater snapped. 'And just remember one thing – I'll be taking even bigger risks than you.' His imperious tone brooked no argument. 'You're still in?'

'You did guarantee a full pardon if we pull this thing off?' The killer appeared coldly calm now yet his eyes bored into Dater's own like twin augers. In that moment he was as dangerous a man as Dater had ever seen.

'Right.'

'Well, in that case I reckon we might do it. . . .'

'Not might. Can and will.'

Dev Vallery paced the high west wing ramparts of the governor's palace, a cigarette between his teeth, eyes restless and quick as he paused to glance down into the gardens lying dim and shadowy beneath a high moon.

He rubbed the back of his neck. It was still there . . . that uneasy feeling that had been troubling him all evening. Several times he'd been prompted to quit the mansion to make a circuit of the city just to assure himself all was well. But each time he'd decided against this, telling himself that in the wake of the slaughter down south it would surely take time to feel normal and slot back back into the rhythms of everyday life.

He grinned.

He was beginning to sound like some ancient Civil War veteran who'd been in battle so long he simply couldn't adjust to peacetime.

He turned inside at the next set of double doors and went looking for Lisa.

And wondered if he should dare propose to her before heading off north to make sure more rustlers hadn't run off with all his cows. . . .

He was still rubbing the back of his neck but was no longer aware of it.

A fleeting shadow darted across the moonlit court-yard towards the corner where the militiaman stood building a cigarette. The six-gun barrel crashed down on the back of the man's head and Sonny Boy caught the slumping body, dragging it back into deep shadows.

His eyes gleaming in the gloomy shadows of the mansion walls, the outlaw waited until a second sentry appeared, pacing slowly past the stables. After he'd passed, Clanton rose from his crouch and went streaking across the open courtyard to gain the sanctuary of the mansion's store-house.

From a deeply recessed doorway he squinted upwards at the lights of the upper floors of the mansion. The governor's headquarters seemed quiet at this late hour with but a few lights showing. He remembered having heard that the palace was usually but lightly guarded owing to the governor's popularity with everybody. Seemed folks figured that if he was so well-liked then nobody would want to harm him.

It felt like tonight had been a long time coming. He knew he'd done wrong many times but it seemed there had always been a reason. It had been a real lousy thing when he kidnapped Lisa, but hadn't he made up for that day when he brought her back, taking hair-raising risks and even turning all his boys against him in the process?

But whether he was right or wrong – whether he was 'Smilin' Sonny Boy' or 'Clanton the mad dog' – he didn't really believe he deserved to be hounded like some wild animal to be slaughtered the way they'd tried to do at Sawtooth Pass.

Or was that just the old Sonny Boy talking – not the changed-for-life man he was this crazy night.

And told himself that, come daybreak, he'd be twenty miles on his way to Mexico.

But he was getting ahead of himself. First, goodbye – then run. Small words, big risk. But worth it . . . just to see her one last time for the rest of his life. Then he would quit with style.

He fingered his gun handle and hoped he wouldn't have to use it, then realized the slow-pacing sentry had passed him by. Next instant he was darting across the echoing quadrangle to vanish into the rear of the servants' quarters on the far side.

Seemingly endless minutes passed with him crouched there in the darkness before a door opened sharply, light flooded out and a scullery hand toting a pail of slops emerged.

The man grunted just once as the gunbutt slammed home. He was lowered silently to the boards and Sonny Boy Clanton was inside the governor's palace.

A short dim corridor stretched ahead. He went to where it intersected a hallway which in turn led to the stairs. His legs were shaking some by the time he'd reached the first floor, but when he looked down at his hand clutching the gun he saw it was rock steady.

On the first floor he was forced to stop and take a swig from his flask. A chink of light showed beneath the third door to his left. He padded across and and placed an ear against it. Somebody was moving about on the other side of the door.

Dater saluted briskly and the tall killer at his side now dressed in militia blue did likewise. The sentry clicked his heels and saluted in response and two men with murder on their minds crossed the quadrangle unhindered and vanished through the doorway of the militia's weapons store.

'Dev, will you please light some place?'

Vallery halted to touch a vesta to his cigarette. He knew he was still edgy and didn't know why. It had been that way all night. He'd tried to relax but found it impossible. Drawing deep on the smoke he wondered if the truth might be that he'd taken one danger ride too far, gunned down one hellion too many?

And visions of his spread with the soft evening light on the hills came clearly and he realized he seemed to be relaxing at long last . . . even if there still seemed to be something in the city night that wasn't just right. . . .

'All right,' Lisa said.

He blinked at her. 'What? I didn't say anything. . . .'

Her smile was forgiving.

'I'm saying . . . all right, please go and take one more walk around the parapets to reassure yourself everything really is all right. Then perhaps we might think about some late supper. I know Father must be starving after such a tumultuous day. Well, what are you waiting for?'

Vallery smiled broadly. She was one in a million. He blew her a kiss and quit the room to head along the corridor and disappeared.

The girl closed the door behind him and turned back to the big room. She didn't see anything untoward at first, but as she moved towards the piano in the corner, the corner of her eye caught a movement.

She turned sharply and her hand flew to her throat.

'Sonny!'

He looked as young and handsome as ever as he stepped from the wall cabinet, smiling boyishly and with hands on hips in a characteristic pose.

'Pleased to see me, Lisa?'

It seemed a weirdly commonplace thing to say considering the sheer unreality of the moment and the girl was at once both reassured and alarmed in the same moment. 'For God's sake, Sonny, you shouldn't be here at this—'

She broke off, started towards him, then paused. There was blood showing on his dark coat and as he moved fully into the light she realized just how pale he appeared. And how his smile seemed fixed in place.

'What are you doing here, Sonny? I thought you were . . . I mean you . . . you're hurt, aren't you?'

'Well, maybe hurt ain't a big enough word . . . all things considered. . . .'

He was moving about the large room, dragging his fingers across the backs of chairs, his eyes seeming too bright against the pallor of his face. Lisa sensed she should be afraid, yet she had never feared this man-boy even when his helpless prisoner.

Yet she did sense the danger when he whirled at a faint sound from the corridor, right hand going to gun handle faster than her eye could follow.

She opened her mouth to cry a warning to whoever it was outside. Before she could do so the door swung inwards and her father entered the room followed by Dev Vallery.

The two froze – and Clanton laughed softly as he motioned with the gun barrel for Vallery to close the door.

'By glory—' Randolph began, but Clanton silenced him with a gesture.

'Better leave me to do the talking . . . folks,' he panted. 'But I've got to say your timing is lousy on account I just wanted to see Lisa private and say goodbye like—'

'How the devil did you get in here?' Randolph broke in. But before he could go farther, Vallery put a hand on his arm then stepped forward as though to protect the older man with his body.

The eyes of one-time friends met and locked in a timeless moment.

'Old pard,' Clanton drawled, yet sounded more puzzled than hurt. He smiled. 'I just planned to see Lisa and tell her something important before I headed for Mexico, Dev. But I'm right glad you showed this way . . . both of you.'

He paused to laugh softly, dominating the room with the gun and with the sheer power of his personality despite his condition. 'Guess you underestimated me but folks have been doing that all my life and—'

He broke off, his free hand grabbing at his side as colour drained from his face. Panther quick, Vallery started towards him. But the .45 jerked up again and

Sonny Boy was smiling no longer.

'I'll get this over with quick,' he panted. 'Lisa, I came here tonight just to tell you I'll love you forever . . . and that I understand why you'd take to a bone-head like old Dev here. . . .'

He coughed and his smile was forced, his eyes too bright. 'I know . . . I only know you really cared for me when we were together in the wilds . . . and I showed how I felt about you by giving you up without any . . . any. . . .'

He swayed and lurched into a centre table. Instantly Vallery lunged for him. Clanton brandished the gun but didn't shoot. Vallery clamped Clanton's gun arm and the two wrestled for possession while Lisa rushed for the door, only to have it burst open and the powerful form of Colonel Dater came charging in trailed by a tall figure also in militia blue.

But this one was no trooper.

Marlon Lord had a big Colt .44 revolver in his hand and his eyes were ice as he angled the weapon towards the governor before Vallery even realized what was happening.

'No!' he roared, and bursting free from Clanton's grip charged at Lord, shoulder jolting Dater from his path.

Watching frozen, Lisa was the only one present with a clear sight of what transpired during that handful of hellish moments that might shape the entire future of Capital City and South-west Territory.

Before Vallery could reach Lord the killer jerked trigger fast. Too fast. The slug scored Dev's shoulder and before Lord could fire again Dev had crash-tackled the gunman, driving him backwards over a settee where the back of his head smashed into the wall with stunning force.

Lord lay sprawled and dazed and Vallery now had drawn his gun as he whirled about on his knees to face Sonny Boy . . . who was smiling down at him with a cocked gun in his fist and a gleam of sweat across his face.

In that moment Vallery reckoned himself a dead man. 'But maybe Sonny wouldn't do it', his mind insisted, and in that fragment of time he swung in profile to Clanton to fix his gunsights on Lord.

And triggered.

The killer seemed to fire in the same instant. Yet it only appeared that way. Dev's shot was a hair's breadth the faster and was on target. Struck between the eyes, Marlon Lord was smashed lifeless into a corner as the last shot he ever fired whined over Vallery's head and smashed a chandelier.

But the big man in the background sliding the heavy cocked .44 from inside his greatcoat unnoticed through the roiling gunsmoke had but one moment to realize it had gone so far now that none but himself must now leave this room alive. In that fragment of time Colonel Nathan Dater reverted to what he had always been deep down. Pure killer.

Lisa's piercing scream distracted Dater for that shaved sliver of a second that saw Sonny Boy whirl and shoot all in the one blurring action – just like the Sonny Boy of old. Struck hard yet still standing, Dater triggered back, the sound of one shot coming hard upon the heels of the other. But a desperate Vallery dived upon his Colt, rolled violently as a six-gun roared deafeningly, then drilled Dater through the heart. The great body was sent slamming against the west wall, there to slide down slowly, seeing nothing, feeling nothing and never hearing the clashing crash of Colts as Vallery and Clanton blasted at each other together, the whole room shuddering to the the slamming blasts as cordite smoke dimmed the light.

Making it to one knee, Dev saw Clanton go reeling back against the heavy desk, yet felt nothing himself. Sonny Boy triggered at him, yet he felt nothing. How could a gun wizard have missed him at point-blank range?

Then the crazy thing. Sonny Boy laughed, then fired again. His bullet ripped into the ceiling and his next drilled harmlessly into a wall.

He was shooting to miss!

'Damnit, Sonny—' he began, but his words chopped off as Clanton turned towards an ashen Lisa, smiled just like the old Sonny, blew her a kiss, then fell almost at her feet.

Shocked and confused, Dev flung his smoking .45 aside and knelt at the dying man's side. A thin trickle of blood ran from the corner of Clanton's mouth, yet he was still smiling just like the Sonny Boy of old.

And all the old charm, affection and love of excitement were in his face as he said. 'Could have got you three times there, Dev. Look on that as my wedding present to you both from me . . . and Sister Kate. . . .'

His words cut off and he fell on his side, lying there like a boy who'd fallen asleep to dream something gentle and fine . . . as Lisa made the sign of the cross and fought back the tears.

For some reason Dev's vision also seemed blurred.

The shootout at the governor's palace finally signalled the end of the violence that had plagued Deaf Smith County for so long. Dater's involvement in that night of blood and death, a mystery at first, was ultimately exposed by the testimony of the militiaman he'd forcefully involved in his attempt to seize power that bloody night.

Within a month the territorial militia was disbanded by presidential decree.

The legend of Sonny Boy Clanton received a tremendous boost with his death and the way he'd averted disaster in his last moments at the governor's palace.

In the printed word he became, over time, in folk-lore and in song, the western counterpart of El Cid or Robin Hood.

His crimes were forgotten, gilded over or disre-garded, while his courage, gun-skill and reckless daring became enshrined in memory. As with most legends, the truth became clouded with time to be moulded and shaped to whatever people wanted to believe. As South-west Territory progressed and pros-pered people remembered the legend but forgot the real man.

But two people did not forget. Each year, on the anniversary of his death, Dev and Lisa Vallery would journey down Split Spur Ranch to visit the cemetery at Capital City. They would lay flowers on the grave of Sonny Boy Clanton and would stand together, remembering the man as they had known him.

Then they would walk slowly away from that small patch of earth, leaving it for another year of rain, searing sun and all the gentle white snows of winter.